THE NAVAL PIONEERS
OF AUSTRALIA

THE NAVAL PIONEERS
OF AUSTRALIA

Copyright © 2006 BiblioBazaar
All rights reserved
ISBN: 1-4264-6556-4

Original copyright: 1899,
LONDON

Louis Becke and Walter Jeffery
AUTHORS OF "A FIRST FLEET FAMILY";
"THE MUTINEER," ETC.

THE NAVAL PIONEERS OF AUSTRALIA

WITH ILLUSTRATIONS

BIBLIOBAZAAR

PREFACE

This book does not pretend to be a history of Australia; it merely gathers into one volume that which has hitherto been dispersed through many. Our story ends where Australian history, as it is generally written, begins; but the work of the forgotten naval pioneers of the country made that beginning possible. Four sea-captains in succession had charge of the penal settlement of New South Wales, and these four men, in laying the foundation of Australia, surmounted greater difficulties than have ever been encountered elsewhere in the history of British colonization. Under them, and by their personal exertions, it was made possible to live upon the land; it was made easy to sail upon the Austral seas. After them came military and civil governors and constitutional government, finding all things ready to build a Greater Britain. Histories there are in plenty, of so many hundred pages, devoted to describing the "blessings of constitutional government," of the stoppage of transportation, of the discovery of gold, and all the other milestones on the road to nationhood; but there is given in them no room to describe the work of the sailors—a chapter or two is the most historians afford the naval pioneers.

The printing by the New South Wales Government of the Historical Records of New South Wales has given bookmakers access to much valuable material (dispatches chiefly) hitherto unavailable; and to the volumes of these Records, to the contemporary historians of "The First Fleet" of Captain Phillip, to the many South Sea "voyages," and other works acknowledged in the text, these writers are indebted. Their endeavour has been to collect together the scattered material that was worth collecting relating to what might be called the naval period of Australia. This involved some years' study and the reading of scores of books, and we mention the fact in extenuation of such faults of commission and omission as may be discerned in the work by the careful student of Australian history.

The authors are very sensible of their obligations to Mr. Emery Walker, not only for the time and trouble which he has bestowed upon the finding of illustrations, but also for many valuable suggestions in connection with the volume.

LOUIS BECKE.

WALTER JEFFERY.

London, 1899.

CONTENTS

CHAPTER I.	INTRODUCTORY—THE EARLIEST AUSTRALIAN VOYAGERS: THE PORTUGUESE, SPANISH, AND DUTCH.	13
CHAPTER II.	DAMPIER: THE FIRST ENGLISHMAN IN AUSTRALIA.	26
CHAPTER III.	CAPTAIN COOK, THE DISCOVERER.	42
CHAPTER IV.	ARTHUR PHILLIP, FOUNDER AND FIRST GOVERNOR OF NEW SOUTH WALES.	59
CHAPTER V.	GOVERNOR HUNTER.	71
CHAPTER VI.	THE MARINES AND THE NEW SOUTH WALES CORPS.	87
CHAPTER VII.	GOVERNOR KING.	100
CHAPTER VIII.	BASS AND FLINDERS.	121
CHAPTER IX.	THE CAPTIVITY OF FLINDERS.	139
CHAPTER X.	BLIGH AND THE MUTINY OF THE "BOUNTY".	155
CHAPTER XI.	BLIGH AS GOVERNOR.	171
CHAPTER XII.	OTHER NAVAL PIONEERS, AND THE PRESENT MARITIME STATE OF AUSTRALIA—CONCLUSION.	190

LIST OF ILLUSTRATIONS

MARTIN FROBISHER 14
FROBISHER'S MAP 15
A DUTCH SHIP OF WAR 22
SOVEREIGN OF THE SEAS 29
A SIXTH RATE, 1684... 34
DAMPIER 38
COOK 44
GOVERNOR PHILLIP.. 62
VIEW OF BOTANY BAY 64
SYDNEY COVE.. 67
CAPTAIN JOHN HUNTER.. 74
ATTACK ON THE WAAKSAMHEYD 79
GOVERNOR KING.. 102
LA PÉROUSE 103
SIR JOSEPH BANKS 114
GEORGE BASS 122
MATTHEW FLINDERS... 124
VIEW OF WRECK REEF... 137
GOVERNMENT HOUSE, SYDNEY, IN 1802..................... 142
VIEW OF SYDNEY 149
GOVERNOR BLIGH.. 177

"Whenever I want a thing well done in a distant part of the world; when I want a man with a good head, a good heart, lots of pluck, and plenty of common sense, I always send for a Captain of the Navy."—LORD PALMERSTON.

CHAPTER I.

INTRODUCTORY—THE EARLIEST AUSTRALIAN VOYAGERS: THE PORTUGUESE, SPANISH, AND DUTCH.

Learned geographers have gone back to very remote times, even to the Middle Ages, and, by the aid of old maps, have set up ingenious theories showing that the Australian continent was then known to explorers. Some evidence has been adduced of a French voyage in which the continent was discovered in the youth of the sixteenth century, and, of course, it has been asserted that the Chinese were acquainted with the land long before Europeans ventured to go so far afloat. There is strong evidence that the west coast of Australia was touched by the Spaniards and the Portuguese during the first half of the sixteenth century, and proof of its discovery early in the seventeenth century. At the time of these very early South Sea voyages the search, it should always be remembered, was for a great Antarctic continent. The discovery of islands in the Pacific was, to the explorers, a matter of minor importance; New Guinea, although visited by the Portuguese in 1526, up to the time of Captain Cook was supposed by Englishmen to be a part of the mainland, and the eastern coast of Australia, though touched upon earlier and roughly outlined upon maps, remained unknown to them until Cook explored it.

MARTIN FROBISHER

1578

Early Voyages to Australia, by R.H. Major, printed by the Hakluyt Society in 1859, is still the best collection of facts and contains the soundest deductions from them on the subject, and although ably-written books have since been published, the industrious authors have added little or nothing in the way of indisputable evidence to that collected by Major. The belief in the existence of the Australian continent grew gradually and naturally out of the belief in a great southern land. Mr. G.B. Barton, in an introduction to his valuable Australian history, traces this from 1578, when Frobisher wrote:—

"Terra Australis seemeth to be a great, firme land, lying under and aboute the south pole, being in many places a fruitefull soyle, and is not yet thorowly discovered, but only seen and touched on the north edge thereof by the travaile of the Portingales and Spaniards in their voyages to their East and West Indies. It is included almost by a paralell, passing at 40 degrees in south latitude, yet in some places it reacheth into the sea with great promontories, even into the tropicke Capricornus. Onely these partes are best known, as over against Capo d' buona Speranza (where the Portingales see popingayes commonly of a wonderful greatnesse), and againe it is knowen at the south side of the straight of Magellanies, and is called Terra del Fuego. It is thoughte this south lande, about the pole Antartike, is farre bigger than the north land about the pole Artike; but whether it be so or not, we have no certaine knowledge, for we have no particular description thereof, as we have of the land under and aboute the north pole."

Then Purchas, in 1678, says:—

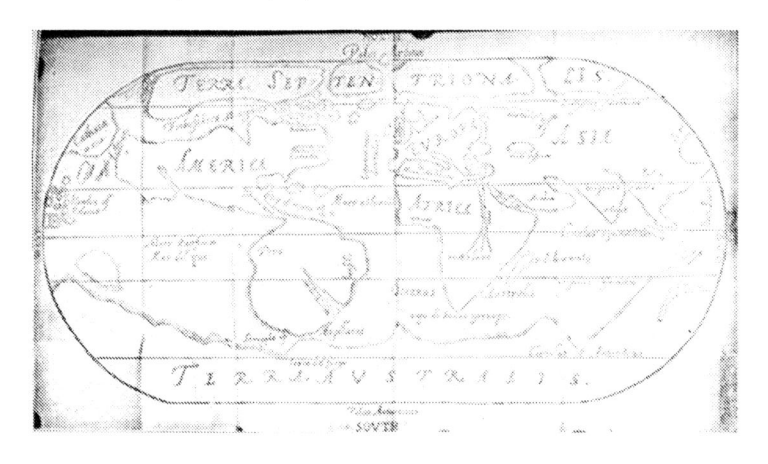

FROBISHER'S MAP

"This land about the Straits is not perfectly discovered, whether it be Continent or Islands. Some take it for Continent, and extend it more in their imagination than any man's experience towards those Islands of Saloman and New Guinea, esteeming (of which there is great probability) that Terra Australis, or the Southerne Continent, may for the largeness thereof take a first place in order and the first in greatnesse in the division and parting of the Whole World."

1605

The most important of the Spanish voyages was that made by De Quiros, who left Callao in December, 1605, in charge of an expedition of three ships. One of these vessels was commanded by Luis Vaez de Torres. De Quiros, who is believed to have been by birth a Portuguese, discovered several island groups and many isolated islands, among the former being the New Hebrides, which he, believing he had found the continent, named Tierra Australis del Espiritu Santo. Soon after the ships commanded by De Quiros became separated from the other vessels, and Torres took charge. He subsequently found that the land seen was an island group, and so determined to sail westward in pursuance of the scheme of exploration. In about the month of August he fell in with a chain of islands (now called the Louisiade Archipelago and included in the British Possession of New Guinea) which he thought, reasonably enough, was the beginning of New Guinea, but which really lies a little to the southeast of that great island. As he could not weather the group, he bore away to the southward, and his subsequent proceedings are here quoted from Burney's *Voyages*:—

"We went along three hundred leagues of coast, as I have mentioned, and diminished the latitude 2-1/2 degrees, which brought us into 9 degrees. From thence we fell in with a bank of from three to nine fathoms, which extends along the coast to 7-1/2 south latitude; and the end of it is in 5 degrees. We could go no further on for the many shoals and great currents, so we were obliged to sail southwest in that depth to 11 degrees south latitude. There is all over it an archipelago of islands without number, by which we passed; and at the end of the eleventh degree the bank became shoaler. Here were very large islands, and they appeared more to the southward. They were inhabited by black people, very corpulent and naked. Their arms were lances, arrows, and clubs of stone ill-fashioned. We could not get any of their arms. We caught in all this land twenty persons of different nations, that with them we might be able to give a better account to your Majesty. They give [us] much notice of other people, although as yet they do not make themselves well understood. We were upon this bank two months, at the end of which time we found ourselves in twenty-five fathoms and 5 degrees south latitude and ten leagues from the coast; and having gone 480 leagues here, the coast goes to the north-east. I did not search it, for the bank became very shallow. So we stood to the north."

The "very large islands" seen by Torres were no doubt the hills of Cape York, the northernmost point of Australia, and so he, all unconsciously, had passed within sight of the continent for which he was searching. A copy of the report by Torres was lodged in the archives of Manila, and when the English took that city in 1762, Dalrymple, the celebrated geographer, discovered it, and gave the name of Torres Straits to what is now well known as the dangerous passage dividing New Guinea from Australia. De Quiros, in his ship, made no further discovery; he arrived on the Mexican coast in October, 1606, and did all he could to induce Philip III. of Spain to sanction further exploration, but without success.

Of the voyages of the Dutch in Australian waters much interesting matter is available. Major sums up the case in these words:—

"The entire period up to the time of Dampier, ranging over two centuries, presents these two phases of obscurity: that in the sixteenth century (the period of the Portuguese and Spanish discoveries) there are indications on maps of the great probability of Australia having already been discovered, but with no written documents to confirm them; while in the seventeenth century there is documentary evidence that its coasts were touched upon or explored by a considerable number of Dutch voyagers, but the documents immediately describing these voyages have not been found."

1644

The period of known Dutch discovery begins with the establishment of the Dutch East India Company, and a knowledge of the west coast of Australia grew with the growth of the Dutch colonies, but grew slowly, for the Dutchmen were too busy trading to risk ships and spend time and money upon scientific voyages.

In January, 1644, Commodore Abel Janszoon Tasman was despatched upon his second voyage of discovery to the South Seas, and his instructions, signed by the Governor-General of Batavia, Antonio Van Diemen, begin with a recital of all previous Dutch voyages of a similar character. From this document an interesting summary of Dutch exploration can be made. Tasman, in his first voyage, had discovered the island of Van Diemen, which he named after the then Governor of Batavia, but which has since been named Tasmania, after its discoverer. During this first voyage the navigator also discovered New Zealand, passed round the east side of Australia without seeing the land, and on his way home sailed along the northern shore of New Guinea.

But to come back to the summary of Dutch voyages found in Tasman's instructions: During 1605 and 1606 the Dutch yacht *Duyphen* made two exploring voyages to New Guinea. On one trip the commander, after coasting New Guinea, steered southward along the islands on the west side of Torres Straits to that part of Australia, a little to the west and south of Cape York, marked on modern maps as Duyphen Point, thus unconsciously—for he thought himself still on the west coast of New Guinea—making the first authenticated discovery of the continent.

1623-1627

Dirk Hartog, in command of the *Endragt*, while on his way from Holland to the East Indies, put into what Dampier afterwards called Sharks' Bay, and on an island, which now bears his name, deposited a tin plate with an inscription recording his arrival, and dated October 25th, 1616. The plate was afterwards found by a Dutch navigator in 1697, and replaced by another, which in its turn was discovered in July, 1801, by Captain Hamelin, of the *Naturaliste*, on the well-known French voyage in search of the ill-fated La Pérouse. The Frenchman copied the inscription, and nailed the plate to a post with another recording his own voyage. These inscriptions were a few years later removed by De Freycinet, and deposited in the museum of the Institute of Paris. Hartog ran along the coast a few degrees, naming the land after his ship, and was followed by many other voyagers at frequent intervals down to the year 1727, from which time Dutch exploration has no more a place in Australian discovery.

During the 122 years of which we have records of their voyages, although the Dutch navigators' work, compared with that done by Cook and his successors, was of small account; yet, considering the state of nautical science, and that the ships were for the most part Dutch East Indiamen, the Dutch names which still sprinkle the north and the west coasts of the continent show that from Cape York in the extreme north, westward of the Great Australian Bight in the south, the Dutchmen had touched at intervals the whole coast-line.

But before leaving the Dutch period there are one or two voyages that, either on account of their interesting or important character, deserve brief mention.

In 1623 Arnhem's Land, now the northern district of the Northern Territory of South Australia, was discovered by the Dutch yachts *Pesa* and *Arnhem*. This voyage is also noteworthy on account of the massacre of the master of the *Arnhem* and eight of his crew by the natives while they were exploring the coast of New Guinea. In 1627 the first discovery of the south coast was made by the *Gulde Zeepard*, and the land then explored, extending from Cape Leeuwin to the Nuyts Archipelago, on the South Australian coast, was named after Peter Nuyts, then on board the ship on his way to Batavia, whence he was sent to Japan as ambassador from Holland.

1629

In the year 1628 a colonizing expedition of eleven vessels left Holland for the Dutch East Indies. Among these ships was the *Batavia*, commanded by Francis Pelsart. A terrible storm destroyed ten of the fleet, and on June 4th, 1629, the *Batavia* was driven ashore on the reef still known as Houtman's Abrolhos, which had been discovered and named by a Dutch East Indiaman some years earlier—probably by the commander of the *Leeuwin,* who discovered and named after his ship the cape at the south-west point of the continent. The *Batavia,* which carried a number of chests of silver money, went to pieces on the reef. The crew of the ship managed to land upon the rocks, and saved some food from the wreck, but they were without water. Pelsart, in one of the ship's boats, spent a couple of weeks exploring the inhospitable coast in the neighbourhood in the hope of discovering water, but found so little that he ultimately determined to attempt to make Batavia and from there bring succour to his ship's company. On July 3rd he fell in with a Dutch ship off Java and was taken on to Batavia. From there he obtained help and returned to the wreck, arriving at the Abrolhos in the middle of September; but during the absence of the commander the castaways had gone through a terrible experience, which is related in Therenot's *Recueil de Voyages Curieux,* and translated into English in Major's book, from which the following is extracted:—

1629

"Whilst Pelsart is soliciting assistance, I will return to those of the crew who remained on the island; but I should first inform you that the supercargo, named Jerome Cornelis, formerly an apothecary at Haarlem, had conspired with the pilot and some others, when off the coast of Africa, to obtain possession of the ship and take her to Dunkirk, or to avail themselves of her for the purpose of piracy. This supercargo remained upon the wreck ten days after the vessel had struck, having discovered no means of reaching the shore. He even passed two days upon the mainmast, which floated, and having from thence got upon a yard, at length gained the land. In the absence of Pelsart, he became commander, and deemed this a suitable occasion for putting his original design into execution, concluding that it would not be difficult to become master of that which remained of the wreck, and to surprise Pelsart when he should arrive with the assistance which he had gone to Batavia to seek, and afterwards to cruise in these seas with his vessel. To accomplish this it was necessary to get rid of those of the crew who were not of his party; but before imbruing his hands with blood he caused his accomplices to sign a species of compact, by which they promised fidelity one to another. The entire crew was divided [living upon] between three islands; upon that of Cornelis, which they had named the graveyard of Batavia, was the greatest number of men. One of them, by name Weybehays, a lieutenant, had been despatched to another island to seek for water, and having discovered some after a search of twenty days, he made the preconcerted signal by lighting three fires, but in vain, for they were not noticed by the people of Cornelis' company, the conspirators having during that time murdered those who were not of their party. Of these they killed thirty or forty. Some few saved themselves upon pieces of wood, which they joined together, and going in search of Weybehays, informed him of the horrible massacre that had taken place. Having with him forty-five men, he resolved to keep upon his guard, and to defend himself from these assassins if they should make an attack upon his company, which in effect they designed to do, and to treat the other party in the same manner; for they feared lest their company, or that which remained upon the third island, should inform the commander upon his arrival, and thus prevent the execution of their design. They succeeded easily with the party last mentioned, which was the weakest, killing the whole of them, excepting seven children and some women. They hoped to succeed as easily with Weybehays' company, and in the meanwhile broke open the chests of merchandise which had been saved from the vessel. Jerome Cornelis caused clothing to be made for his company out of the rich stuffs which he found therein, choosing to himself a bodyguard, each of whom he clothed in scarlet, embroidered with gold and silver. Regarding the women as part of the spoil, he took one for himself, and gave one of the daughters of the minister to a principal member of his party, abandoning the other three for public use. He drew up also certain rules for the future conduct of his men.

A DUTCH SHIP OF WAR

"After these horrible proceedings he caused himself to be elected captain-general by a document which he compelled all his companions to sign. He afterwards sent twenty-two men in two shallops to destroy the company of Weybehays, but they met with a repulse. Taking with him thirty-seven men, he went himself against Weybehays, who received him at the water's edge as he disembarked, and forced him to retire, although the lieutenant and his men had no weapons but clubs, the ends of which were armed with spikes. Finding force unavailing, the mutineer had recourse to other means. He proposed a treaty of peace, the chaplain, who remained with Weybehays, drawing up the conditions. It was agreed to with this proviso, that Weybehays' company should remain unmolested, and they, upon their part, agreed to deliver up a little boat in which one of the sailors had escaped from the island where Cornelis was located to that of Weybehays, receiving in return some stuffs for clothing his people. During his negotiations Cornelis wrote to certain French soldiers who belonged to the lieutenant's company offering to each a sum of money to corrupt them, with the hope that with this assistance he might easily compass his design. His letters, which were without effect, were shown to Weybehays, and Cornelis, who was ignorant of their disclosure, having arrived the next day with three or four others to find Weybehays and bring him the apparel, the latter caused him to be attacked, killed two or three of the company, and took Cornelis himself prisoner. One of them, by name Wouterlos, who escaped from this rout, returned the following day to renew the attack, but with little success.

1629

"Pelsart arrived during these occurrences in the frigate *Sardam*. As he approached the wreck he observed smoke from a distance, a circumstance that afforded him great consolation, since he perceived by it that his people were not all dead. He cast anchor, and threw himself immediately into a skiff with bread and wine, and proceeded to land on one of the islands. Nearly at the same time a boat came alongside with four armed men. Weybehays, who was one of the four, . . . informed him of the massacre, and advised him to return as speedily as possible to his vessel, for that the conspirators designed to surprise him, having already murdered twenty-five persons, and to attack him with two shallops, adding that he himself had that morning been at close quarters with them. Pelsart perceived at the same time the two shallops coming towards him, and had scarcely got on board his own vessel before they came alongside. He was surprised to see the people covered with embroidery of gold and silver and weapons in their hands, and demanded of them why they approached the vessel armed. They replied that they would inform him when they came on board. He commanded them to cast their arms into the sea, or otherwise he would sink them. Finding themselves compelled to submit, they threw away their weapons, and being ordered on board, were immediately placed in irons. One of them, named Jan de Bremen, confessed that he had put to death or assisted in the assassination of twenty-seven persons. The same evening Weybehays brought his prisoner on board.

"On the 18th day of September the captain and the master-pilot, taking with them ten men of Weybehays' company, passed over in boats to the island of Cornelis. Those who still remained thereon lost all courage as soon as they saw them, and allowed themselves to be placed in irons."

Pelsart remained another week at the Abrolhos, endeavouring to recover some of the *Batavia's* treasure, and succeeded in finding all but one chest. The mutineers were tried by the officers of the *Sardam*, and all but two were executed before the ship left the scene of their awful crime. The two men who were not hanged were put on shore on the mainland, and were probably the first Europeans to end their lives upon the continent. Dutch vessels for many years afterwards sought for traces of the marooned seamen, but none were ever discovered.

The 1644 voyage of Tasman was made expressly for the purpose of exploring the north and north-western shores of the continent, and to prove the existence or otherwise of straits separating it from New Guinea. Tasman's instructions show this, and prove that while the existence of the straits was suspected, and although Torres had unconsciously passed through them, they were not known. Tasman explored a long length of coast-line, establishing its continuity from the extreme north-western point (Arnhem Land) as far as the twenty-second degree of south latitude (Exmouth Gulf). He failed to prove the existence of Torres Straits, but to him, it is generally agreed, is due the discovery and naming of the Gulf of Carpentaria (Carpenter in Tasman's time being President at Amsterdam of the Dutch East India Company) and the naming of a part of North Australia, as he had previously named the island to the south, after Van Diemen. From this voyage dates the name New Holland: the great stretch of coast-line embracing his discoveries became known to his countrymen as Hollandia Nova, a name which in its English form was adopted for the whole continent, and remained until it was succeeded by the more euphonious name of Australia. Tasman continued doing good service for the Dutch East India Company until his death at Batavia about 1659.

1727

The last Dutch voyage which space permits us to mention briefly is that of the *Zeewigk*, which ship was wrecked on the Abrolhos in 1727, with a quantity of treasure on board. Some of the crew built a sloop out of the wreck and made their way to Batavia, taking with them the bulk of the treasure; but from time to time, even down to the present century, relics of the wreck, including several coins, have been recovered, and are now to be seen in the museum of the West Australian capital. But before the Dutch had given up exploring the coast of New Holland, Dampier, the first Englishman to set foot upon its shores, had twice visited the continent, and with his two voyages the English naval story of Australia may properly begin.

CHAPTER II.

DAMPIER: THE FIRST ENGLISHMAN IN AUSTRALIA.

"I dined with Mr. Pepys, where was Captain Dampier, who had been a famous buccaneer, had brought hither the painted Prince Job, and printed a relation of his very strange adventure and his observations. He was now going abroad again by the King's encouragement, who furnished a ship of 290 tons. He seemed a more modest man than one would imagine by the relation of the crew he had consorted with. He brought a map of his observations of the course of the winds of the South Sea, and assured us that the maps hitherto extant were all false as to the Pacific Sea, which he makes on the south of the line, that on the north and running by the coast of Peru being I exceedingly tempestuous."

Thus wrote John Evelyn on August 6th, 1698.

Of the adventurous career of Dampier prior to this date too much fiction and quite enough history has already been written; but we cannot omit a short account of the buccaneer's life up to the time of his receiving King William's commission.

1673-1698

Dampier was born in 1652 at East Coker, Somersetshire. Of his parents he tells us that "they did not originally design me for the sea, but bred me at school till I came of years fit for a trade. But upon the death of my mother they who had the disposal of me took other measures, and, having removed me from the Latin school to learn writing and arithmetic, they soon placed me with a master of a ship at Weymouth, complying with the inclinations I had very early of seeing the world."

Dampier made several voyages in merchantmen; then he shipped as able seaman on the *Royal Prince*, Captain Sir Edward Spragge, and served under him till the death of that commander at the end of the Dutch war in 1673. Soon after he made a voyage to the West Indies; then began an adventurous life—ashore cutting logwood in the Bay of Campeachy when not fighting; afloat a buccaneer—of which he has given us details in his *Voyage round the Terrestrial Globe*.

In March, 1686, Dampier in a little barque, the *Cygnet*, commanded by Captain Swan, quitted the American coast and sailed westward across the Pacific. On this voyage the *Cygnet* touched at the Ladrones, the Bashee Islands, the Philippines, Celebes, Timor, New Holland, and the Nicobar Islands. Here Dampier left his ship and worked his way to England, which he reached in 1691. (The *Cygnet* was afterwards lost off Madagascar.) He had brought home with him from Mindanao a tattooed slave, whom he called the "Painted Prince Jeoey," and who was afterwards exhibited as the first painted savage ever seen in England. "Jeoey," who died at Oxford, is the "painted Prince Job" mentioned by Evelyn.

It has been stated that the *Cygnet* touched at New Holland. This land was sighted on January 4th, 1688, in what Dampier says was "latitude 16·50 S. About three leagues to the eastward of this point there is a pretty deep bay, with abundance of islands in it, and a very; good place to anchor in or to haul ashore. About a league to the eastward of that point we anchored January the 5th, 1688, two miles from the shore."

A modern map of West Australia will show the West Kimberley goldfield. To the west of the field is the district of West Kimberley, and upon the coast-line is the Buccaneer Archipelago. The bay in which Dampier anchored is still called Cygnet Bay, and it is situated in the north-west corner of King's Sound, of which "that point" to which "we went a league to the eastward" is named Swan Point, while a rock called Dampier's Monument more particularly commemorates the buccaneer's visit.

The ship remained in Cygnet Bay until March 12th, and during that time the vessel was hove down and repaired. Dampier's observations on the aboriginal inhabitants during his stay is summed up in his description of the natives whom he saw, and who were, he says, "the most miserable people in the world. The Hodmadods" (Hottentots) "of Monomatapa, though a nasty people, yet for wealth are gentlemen to these." He gives an accurate description of the country so far as he saw it, and asserts that "New Holland is a very large tract of land. It is not yet determined whether it is an island or a main continent; but I am certain that it joins neither Asia, Africa, nor America."

While the ship was being overhauled under the sweltering rays of a tropical sun, the men lived on shore in a tent, and Dampier, who was tired of the voyage, probably because there were no Spaniards to fight and no prizes to be made, endeavoured to persuade his companions to shape their next course for some port where was an English factory; but they would not listen to him, and for his pains he was threatened that when the ship was ready for sea he should be landed and left behind.

Evelyn tells us that in 1698 Dampier was going abroad again by the King's commission, and this second voyage of the ex-buccaneer to the South Seas, although of small importance to geographers, is noteworthy, inasmuch as Dampier's was the first visit of a ship of the English royal navy to Australian seas.

To understand what sort of an expedition was this of two hundred years ago, how Dampier was equipped and what manner of ship and company he commanded, it will not be out of place to give some account of the navy at that time. When James II. abdicated in 1688, according to Pepys, the royal navy was made up of 173 ships of 101,892 tons, an armament of 6930 guns, and 42,003 men. William died in 1702, and the number of ships had then increased to 272, and the tonnage to 159,020 tons.

The permanent navy, begun by Henry VIII. and given its first system of regular warfare by the Duke of York in 1665, had become well established, and trading vessels had ceased to form a part of the regular establishment. King William III., although not so good a friend to the service as his predecessor, and anything but a sailor, like the fourth William, did not altogether neglect it. In the Introduction to James' *Naval History* we are told that between the years 1689 and 1697 the navy lost by capture alone 50 vessels, and it is probable that an equal number fell by the perils of the sea. King William meantime added 30 ships, and half that number were captured from the French, while several 20 and 30-gun ships were besides taken from the enemy.

Coming back to the first naval expedition to Australia, the ship commanded by Dampier was the *Roebuck*, as Evelyn tells us, a vessel of 290 tons. Dampier has left very little description of his ship, but it is not difficult to picture her, for by this time the ratings of ships had been settled upon certain lines, and the meaning of the word "rating" as used at this period is easily ascertainable.

According to Charnock's *Marine Architecture*, the *Roebuck*, lying at Deptford in June, 1684, was a sixth-rate of 24 guns and 85 men. This was her war complement; but Dampier himself tells us that he "sailed from the Downs early on Saturday, January 14th, 1699, with a fair wind, in His Majesty's ship the *Roebuck*, carrying but 12 guns on this voyage and 50 men with 20 months' provisions."

SOVEREIGN OF THE SEAS

In 1677, according to James' *History*, the smallest fifth-rate then afloat corresponds nearest to the *Roebuck*, and, no doubt, by

Dampier's time this vessel had been reduced in her rating. The vessel of 1677 is described as being of 265 tons and 28 guns, "sakers and minions," with a complement of about 100 men. The largest sixth-rate was 199 tons, 18 guns, and 85 men. So from these particulars we can take it as correct that the *Roebuck* in 1699 was a sixth-rate. It is worth remembering that in Cavendish's second expedition to the South Sea, in 1591, there was a ship called the *Roebuck*, commanded by John Davis, and likely enough the sixth-rate in which Dampier sailed was named after her, those who gave her the name little thinking at the time of her christening (she was built before Dampier's voyage, and was certainly not the *Roebuck* of Cavendish's fleet) how appropriately they were naming her for her future service.

Her armament is a matter of interest, for just about her time—that is, between the years 1685 and 1716—the naming of guns after beasts and birds of prey went out of fashion, and they were distinguished by the weight of the shot fired. James, quoting from Sir William Monson's *Naval Tracts*, supplies the following table on the subject of sea guns; and, as they were probably still in use in Dampier's time, we print it here:—

Names.	Bore of cannon in inches.	Weight of cannon in pounds.	Weight of shot in pounds	Weight of powder in pounds.
Cannon-royal	8-1/2	8000	66	30
Cannon	8	6000	60	27
Cannon-serpentine	7	5500	53-1/2	25
Bastard cannon	7	4500	41	20
Demi-cannon	6-3/4	4000	33-1/2	18
Cannon-petro	6	4000	24-1/2	14
Culverin	5-1/2	4500	17-1/2	12
Basilisk	5	4000	15	10
Demi-culverin	4	3400	9-1/2	8
Bastard culverin	4	3000	5	5-3/4
Sakers	3-1/2	1400	5-1/2	5-1/2
Minion	3-1/2	1000	4	4
Falcon	2-1/2	660	2	3-1/2
Falcone	2	500	1-1/2	3
Serpentine	1-1/2	400	3/4	1-3/4
Rabinet	1	300	1/2	1/2

The small arms were matchlocks, snaphainces, musketoons, blunderbusses, pistols, halberts, swords, and hangers.

From this it will be seen that the *Roebuck's* guns, considering the peaceful service she was upon, were probably known to her company as "sakers" and "falcons."

In a sixth-rate the sakers were carried all on the one deck, and the minions on the quarterdeck. Charnock supplies an illustration of a sixth-rate of the time, and the picture is a familiar one to all who have taken even a slight interest in the ships of a couple of centuries ago. A lion rampant decorates the stem, set as it remained till early in the present century (the galley prow had gone with Charles I.); the hull looked not a whit more clumsy than that of an old north-country collier of our youth, but the flat stern, with its rows of square windows, richly carved panelling, and big stern-lanterns, and the row of round gun-ports encircled by gold wreaths along the ship's sides, are distinctive marks of this period.

A vessel of this kind was ship-rigged, about 88 feet long by 24 feet beam; the depth of her hold, in which to store her twenty months' provisions (a marvellously large quantity as stores were then carried), was about 11 feet, and her draught of water when loaded about 12 feet aft. She had one deck and a poop and forecastle, the former extending from either end of the ship to the waist. A good deal of superfluous ornament had by this time been done away with, although there was plenty of it so late as 1689. Charnock describes a man-of-war of that date. After the Restoration, ships grew apace in grandeur in and out. Inboard they were painted a dull red (this was, it is said, so that in fighting the blood of the wounded should not show), outside blue and gilded in the upper parts, then yellow, and last black to the water-line, with white bottoms. Copper sheathing had not come into use, and ships' bottoms were treated with tallow, which was made to adhere by being laid on between nails which studded the bottom.

The pitching of the vessels imperilled the masts of these somewhat cranky ships of 1689, says a writer of about Dampier's time, who also tells us that ships then had awnings, and that "glass lanthorns were worthier best made of crystal horn; lanthorns were worthier than isinglass."

The sails were the usual courses: big topsails and topgallantsails, staysails, and topmastsails, with a spritsail and a lateen-mizen; the spanker and jib were not yet, but the sprit-topsail had just gone out. The ship when rigged and fitted ready for sea probably cost King William's Admiralty about £10,000. But the *Roebuck* was pretty well worn out when Dampier was given the command of her, as he tells us when relating her subsequent loss.

The British Fleet, by Commander C.N. Robinson, is an invaluable book to the student of naval history, and, notwithstanding plenty of book authorities and ten years' study of the subject, the present writers are compelled to draw upon Commander Robinson for many details. With the aid of this work and from allusions to be found in the writings of a couple of centuries ago, it is possible to make some sort of picture of Dampier's companions in the *Roebuck*.

Dampier himself was a type of naval officer who entered the service of the country by what was then, and remained for many years afterwards, one of the best sources of supply. He had been given a fair education, and had been duly apprenticed and learned the profession of a sailor in a merchant ship. Upon his return from his first voyage to the South Seas he published an account of his travels, and dedicated it to the President of the Royal Society, the Hon. Charles Mountague, who, appreciating the author's zeal and his intelligent public spirit, recommended him to the patronage of the Earl of Oxford, then Principal Lord of the Admiralty. Dampier's dedication has nothing of the fulsome flattery and begging-letter style so often the chief characteristic of such compositions, but is the straightforward offer of a humble worker in science of the best of his work to the man best able to appreciate and to make the most of it. Dampier's dedication led to his appointment in the navy, and the transaction does honour to both the patron and him who was patronized.

As is well known, until comparatively recent times only the officers of the fighting branch held commissions; all others were either warrant or petty officers. In the time of William III., a captain and one lieutenant were allowed to each ship, and none of the other officers held commissions. The peaceful mission of the *Roebuck* justifies us in concluding that Dampier held the King's commission as a lieutenant commanding, and he was probably given a lieutenant to take charge in case of accident, a master, a couple of master's mates, a gunner, a boatswain and carpenter, and the usual petty officers; seamen and boys made up the complement. Dampier's pay, so far as we can ascertain, would be at the rate of about £12 per month.

Two regiments of marine infantry had been formed so early as 1689, but they were disbanded nine years later. It was not until 1703 that the marines, all infantry, became a permanent branch of the service.

Uniforms had not even been thought of at this time, and the *Roebuck's* officers, from her commander downwards, ate and drank and clothed themselves in much the same fashion as their men. Dampier probably had a room right aft under the long poop, and the other officers at the same end of the ship in canvas-partitioned cabins, the fore part of her one living deck being occupied by the crew. There was probably a mess-room under the poop common to all the officers. What they had to eat and drink, as we have said, was the same for all ranks. Here is a scale of provisions for eighty-five men of a sixth-rate of 1688 for two months, taken from Charnock:—

		Tons	cwts.	qrs.	lbs.
Beer	(each man a wine gallon per day)	17	0	0	0
Bread	(" 1 lb. per day)	2	2	1	0
Beef	(" 4 " week)	1	4	0	0
Pork	(" 2 " ")	0	12	0	16
Pease	(" 2 pints per week)	0	12	0	16
Oatmeal	(" 3 " ")[A]	0	13	2	18
Butter	(" 6 oz. per week)	0	2	3	
Cheese	(" 12 " ")	0	4	2	6
Water	(in iron-bound casks)	7	0	0	0

In 1690 flour and raisins were added, and an effort made to condense water. Beer took the place of all forms of drink, and water was at that time carried in casks.

The dress, from contemporary prints, can be easily made out, and the allusions of Pepys and Evelyn supply the names and

---

[A] In lieu of three eighths of a fish.

materials of the garments. Pepys' diary and letters inform us how the pursers of the time supplied the men with slops, and in *The British Fleet* considerable detail on this subject is given. Roughly it may be assumed that Dampier's sailors wore petticoats and breeches, grey kersey jackets, woollen stockings and low-heeled shoes, and worsted, canvas, or leather caps. Canvas, leather, and coarse cloth were the principal materials, and tin buttons and coloured thread the most ornamental part, of the costume. Charnock says that in 1663 "sailors began first to wear distinctive dress. A rule was that only red caps, yarn and Irish stockings, blue shirts, white shirts, cotton waistcoats, cotton drawers, neat leather flat-heeled shoes, blue neckcloths, canvas suits, and rugs were to be sold to them. Red breeches were worn."

Smollett's pictures of the service in *Roderick Random*, written forty years after Dampier's time, give us some idea of life on board ship, for in the forty years between the two dates it differed in no essential particulars. Pepys describes a sailor who had lost his eye in action having the socket plugged with oakum, a fact which tells more than could a volume of how seamen were then cared for. It was the days of the press and of the advance-note system, which prevailed well into the present century, and those seamen who went with Dampier of their own free will on a voyage where nothing but the poorest pay and no prize money was to be got were probably the lowest and most ill-disciplined rascals, drawn from a class upon whose characters, save for their bulldog courage and reckless prodigality, the least written the better.

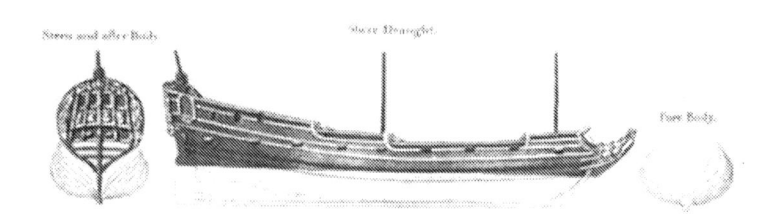

A SIXTH RATE, 1684

The modern bluejacket, superior in every respect, notwithstanding certain croakers, is infinitely better than his ancestors in the very quality which was their best; the modern sailor faces death soberly and decently in forms far more terrible than were ever dreamt of by his forefathers. When the *Calliope* steamed out of Apia Harbour in the hurricane of March, 1889, the youngest grimy coal-trimmer, whose sole duty it was to silently shovel coal, even though his last moment came to him while doing it, never once asked if the ship was making way. All hands in this department were on duty for sixteen hours, and during that time no sound was heard, save the ring of the shovels firing the boilers, nor was a question asked by any man as to the progress of the ship or the chances of life and death.

Compare this end-of-the-century story with that of the loss of the *Wager*, one of the ships of Anson's squadron; and compare the behaviour of the *Wager's* castaways with that of the bluejackets who stood to attention on the deck of the *Victoria* till the word was given to jump as the ship heeled over—recent instances quoted merely because they occur to the writers' minds, for there are any number of others. Such cases illustrate forcibly this truth: we have, by careful training of the modern sailor, added to the traditional bravery of the class a quality, not lacking, but never properly developed, in the old type, that is, the dignity of coolness and self-restraint, the perfect control of men in the supreme moments of excitement and death.

Dampier's men, from a very early stage in his voyage, were a trouble to him. Two only of them, he says, had ever crossed the line, and he was in continual fear of some sickness arising because they were too lazy to shift themselves, but would lie in their hammocks in wet clothes. Three months after the ship got to sea, when nearing Brazil, he tells us that

> "the disorders in my ship made me think at present that Pernambuco would not be so fit a place for me, being told that ships ride there two or three leagues from the town, under the command of no forts; so that whenever I should have been ashore it might have been easy for my discontented crew to have cut or slipt their cables, and have gone away from me, many of them discovering already an intention to return to England, and some of them declaring openly that they would go no further onwards than Brazil. I altered my course, therefore, and stood away from Bahio

> de todos los Santos, or the Bay of All Saints, where I hoped to have the governor's help, if need should require, for securing my ship from any such mutinous attempt, being forced to keep myself all the way upon my guard and to lie with my officers, such as I could trust, and with small arms, upon the quarterdeck, it scarce being safe for me to lie in my cabin, by reason of the discontents among my men."

Similar instances of the ill-discipline of the ship are given at intervals throughout Dampier's account of his voyage, and the commander and his officers were all on bad terms with each other, which, however, so far as can be judged now, was, in some degree, the fault of Dampier's uncertain temper.

The scientific results of the *Roebuck's* voyage were, chiefly on these accounts, of no great importance, judged by the standard of such work today; but, with the state of nautical science at the time, not much was to be expected in the way of accurate surveying.

When Dampier set out to explore the coast of New Holland, what charts, what instruments, what scientific knowledge and equipment, had he for the work?

Dampier's time was distinctively an intermediate period. Little more than a century had elapsed since Gerard Mercator's chart was published, and Edward Wright had taught its true principles, and about half a century before the voyage of the *Roebuck* such improvements as Gunter's application of logarithms to nautical calculations, middle latitude sailing, and the measurement of a degree on the meridian were introduced. Hadley's quadrant came thirty years after Dampier, who must have used Davis' instrument, then about ninety years old. Davis' work on navigation, with Wright's chart showing the northern extremity of Australia, and Addison's *Arithmetical Navigation* (1625) were, no doubt, text-books on board the *Roebuck*. Longitude by chronometer was to come half a century after Dampier was in his grave, and such charts as he possessed did little more than indicate the existence of Terra Australis. The Portuguese, Spanish, and Dutch maps were not easy for Englishmen to procure, and all that Dampier has to say on the matter is:—

> "But in the draught that I had of this coast, which was Tasman's, it was laid down in 19 degrees, and the shore

is laid down as joining in one body or continent, with some openings appearing like rivers, and not like islands, as really they are ... This place, therefore, lies more northerly by 40 minutes than is laid down in Mr. Tasman's draught, and besides its being made a firm, continued land, only with some openings like the mouths of rivers, I found the soundings also different from what the line of his course shows them, and generally shallower than he makes them, which inclines me to think that he came not so near the shore as his line shows, and so had deeper soundings, and could not so well distinguish the islands. His meridian or difference of longitude from Sharks' Bay agrees well enough with my account, which is 232 leagues, though we differ in latitude. And, to confirm my conjecture that the line of his course is made too near the shore, at least not so far to the east of this place, the water is there so shallow that he could not come there so nigh."

1638-1697

That the narrative of Tasman's voyage was at that time in existence there is little doubt, and an outline of the coasts visited by him was given in an atlas presented to Charles II. of England, in 1660, by Klencke, of Amsterdam, and now in the British Museum. Major also found in the British Museum copies of charts and a quantity of MS. describing Tasman's 1644 voyage, which, there is reason to believe, were made from Tasman's originals by one Captain Bowrey in 1688, who had spent fourteen years before that date trading in the Dutch East Indies. These documents are all that have been found, and a diligent search of geographers still leaves undiscovered Tasman's original narrative. The 1688 copies were probably known to Dampier when he sailed in the *Roebuck*, and he was, likely enough, supplied with specially made duplicates by the naval authorities. In 1697 a translation of a French book was published in England by John Dunton, of the Poultry, London, with the title *A New Discovery of Terra Incognita Australis, or the Southern World, by James Sadeur, a Frenchman*. The Frenchman told a story of thirty-five years' adventures in New Holland; but his tale was a lie from beginning to end. Coming so close to the date of Dampier's voyage, it is worth noting that he does not allude to the book, and so probably, notwithstanding the little knowledge Englishmen then had of the southern continent, Dampier was shrewd enough to detect the imposture.

The *Roebuck* struck soundings on the night of August 1st, 1699, upon the northern part of the Abrolhos. Dampier then cautiously ran northward, keeping the land in sight until he anchored in Dirk Hartog's Road, in a sound which he named Sharks' Bay, for the reason that his men caught and ate, among other things, many sharks, including one eleven feet long, and says Dampier, "Our men eat them very savorilly." He gives us, too, a description of the kangaroo, the first introduction of that animal to civilization. Says the navigator, "The land animals that we saw here were only a sort of racoons, different from those of the West Indies, chiefly as to their legs; for these have very short fore legs, but go jumping upon them as the others do, and, like them, are very good meat."

DAMPIER

To face p. 38.

1699

Sharks' Bay is in what is now called the Gascoyne division of West Australia, after the river of that name. Its chief town is Carnarvon, situated at the mouth of the river. Wool-growing is the principal industry, and the population is about 800.

Dampier stayed eight days in the bay, then ran northward along the coast, discovering the archipelago named after him, and himself naming Rosemary Island, which lies off the coast close to Roeburne, the chief town of the north province of the colony. From here he continued his course north till he reached Roebuck Bay, a few leagues to the south of the scene of his first visit, and where is now the town of Broome. The Eastern Extension Telegraph Cable Company's alternative cable from Banjoewangi comes in here, and the town has additional importance as being the harbour for a large pearling fleet.

Dampier left here on September 5th, intending again to land further north, but he abandoned the idea and directed his course for Timor. After he left Timor he called at New Guinea, discovered and named New Britain, now a German colonial possession, spent some weeks upon the New Guinea coast, and then returned to Timor, whence he began his voyage home. Off Ascension the *Roebuck* sprang a leak and foundered. Her company, who with difficulty saved their lives, landed upon Ascension, where they remained till they were rescued and brought to England in the *Canterbury*, East Indiaman.

During his stay on the coast of New Guinea Dampier, besides those discoveries already enumerated, made others, and the frequent appearance of his name on a modern chart of this coast still commemorates them.

Of Dampier's personality his writings give us little insight. As a good writer should, he keeps his private affairs out of his book, but how much we should have been interested in knowing something of the man's shore life! Mr. Clark Russell in his admirable sketch of Dampier, for example, takes it for granted that he never married, at any rate during his sea career. Dampier himself tells us he was married, and gives us a very good idea of when, but he so seldom, after once getting to work upon his narrative, gives us a glimpse of himself that it is easily understood how Mr. Russell came to miss that passage in the *Voyage round the World* in which the old sailor tells us how in 1687 he named an island the Duke of Grafton's Isle "as soon as we all landed on it, having married my wife out of the Duchess's family and leaving her at Arlington House at my going abroad."

He was, perhaps, not a great man, though a good sailor, who had certain qualities which placed him above his fellows. We imagine somehow that his expressed pious dislike for buccaneering was not altogether the cause of his abandoning the life, and that when he set out upon his career as an explorer the search for a land where gold could be easily got without fighting for it was his main motive. He himself tells us so, but we think that he might have been a greater man if his mind had been capable of a little higher aim than the easy getting of riches. The obscurity of his end is not remarkable when one considers how little was then thought of the value of his discoveries. It took many years for Cook's survey of New Holland to bring forth fruits.

In his third volume, written after his return from Ascension, he says:—

> "It has always been the fate of those who have made new discoveries to be disesteemed and slightly spoken of by such as either have had no true relish and value for the things themselves that are discovered, or have had some prejudice against the persons by whom the discoveries were made. It would be vain, therefore, and unreasonable in me to expect to escape the censure of all, or to hope for better treatment than far worthier persons have met with before me. But this satisfaction I am sure of having, that the things themselves in the discovery of which I have been employed are most worthy of our diligent search and inquiry, being the various and wonderful works of God in different parts of the world; and, however unfit a person I may be in other respects to have undertaken this task, yet, at least, I have given a faithful account, and have found some things undiscovered by any before, and which may at least be some assistance and direction to better qualified persons who shall come after me."

This is a very fair summary of his work, and in his dedication of his book to the Earl of Pembroke he says truly enough:—

> "The world is apt to judge of everything by its success; and whoever has ill-fortune will hardly be allowed a good name. This, my lord, was my unhappiness in my late expedition in the *Roebuck*, which foundered through perfect age near the island of Ascension. I suffered extremely in my reputation by that misfortune, though I comfort myself with the thoughts that my enemies could not charge any neglect upon me."

1715

Upon his return from the *Roebuck* voyage his next exploit was the command of a privateering expedition consisting of the *St. George* and the *Cinque Ports*, equipped by a company to cruise against the Spaniards in the South Seas. He sailed upon this voyage in April, 1703, first having the honour of a presentation by the Lord High Admiral to the new Queen (Anne). It is well known that the voyage was a failure, and how Dampier, in command of the *St. George*, quarrelled with Funnel, in command of the *Cinque Ports*. After this voyage he began his downward career, and the next heard of him is when he sailed as pilot on the well-known Woodes Rogers expedition, returning in 1711 a very small sharer in booty to the value of about £150,000.

It was on this voyage that Alexander Selkirk was found upon Juan Fernandez, and Woodes Rogers learned from his pilot, Captain Dampier, how the man had been left upon the island more than four years before from the *Cinque Ports*, and that Selkirk was the best man in her, and so Rogers took him on board his ship.

This, so far as written story goes, is the last of Dampier, and nothing is known of how he spent his declining days. The discovery of his will proves that he died in Coleman Street, St. Stephen's, London, some time in 1715. The will does not mention the value of his property, but he could not have died rich, and was probably not only poor, but, to judge by the fact of his death not having been recorded by his contemporaries, must have been almost, so far as the great folks who once patronized him were concerned, friendless.

CHAPTER III.

CAPTAIN COOK, THE DISCOVERER.

1755

From Dr. Hawkesworth's pedantic volumes to Sir Walter Besant's delightful sketch, there are any number of versions of the story of Cook's life and work. Let us assume that everyone knows how James Cook, son of a superior farm labourer in Yorkshire, at thirteen years of age apprenticed to a fishing village shopkeeper, ran away to sea in a Whitby collier, and presently got himself properly apprenticed to her owners, two Quaker brothers named Walker, and how at twenty-seven years of age, when he had become mate of a small merchantman, he determined to anticipate the hot press of May, 1755, and so at Wapping volunteered as A.B. on board His Majesty's ship *Eagle*.

His knowledge of navigation and his good conduct led to such recognition that when he was under thirty he was appointed master of the *Mercury*. His surveying work on the St. Lawrence at the siege of Quebec was so carried out that the Admiralty saw in him one of the most promising officers in the service; and Sir Hugh Palliser, one of the first men to "discover" Cook, was from this time, his best friend, giving him, in 1764, an appointment as marine surveyor of Newfoundland, where Palliser was governor. Cook was then a good seaman and a clever navigator, but there is no doubt his special talents were by this particular service afforded an opportunity for full development, and so he became the best scientific man in the navy. In 1769 it was determined to send an expedition to the Pacific to observe the transit of Venus. Cook had just returned from Newfoundland, and he was appointed to the command.

Seventy years had elapsed since Dampier's voyage in the *Roebuck*. Meanwhile what had the English done in the way of South Sea exploration? What was the navy like at this time, a year before Nelson, a youngster of twelve, first went to sea?

1769

There are books enough in print to reply to these questions; but with how much more interest could they be answered if the newspaper press, with its interviewers and its photo-reproductions, had been then what it is now. To put life into the skeleton histories, to give us sea life as it was and sailors as they were, we have to trust mostly to the novelists, who, except in rare instances, draw untrustworthy exaggerations.

No doubt there are families who have, so to speak, specialized their traditions for generations; and a naval family's traditions for the last two centuries would make a most entertaining book. Suppose, for instance, there were living at Portsmouth a man whose family for generations had prided itself on some one of its members having shaken hands with all the great sailors who at some time or other in their careers must have sailed from Spithead. This man could tell us how his father had actually shaken hands with Nelson.

There died in February, 1898, in Melbourne, Australia, Lieutenant Pascoe, son of Nelson's flag-lieutenant at Trafalgar, so that the first proposition is established. Now Nelson's Pascoe could easily have been patted on the head by Cook, and the father of any of Cook's men could easily have sailed with Dampier. Looked at in this way, it does not seem difficult to span the gulfs between each of these naval epochs, and if one compares Dampier's *Roebuck* and her crew with Cook's *Endeavour* and her crew and with the ships and seamen of Nelson's time, it still seems easy enough; but between us and them steam and iron have come, and we are as far apart from those others as the Martians are from us.

At the time when Cook started on his voyage England had for several years been engaged in, and was almost constantly at, naval war. From the French and Spanish prizes we got many valuable hints in the designing of ships, and our builders improved upon them with the best workmanship and materials in the world, so that the warships of Cook's time differed little from, and in many cases were, the hulks which, until very recent years, lay in our naval seaports. It ought not to be necessary to remind readers that Nelson's *Victory*, still afloat in Portsmouth harbour, was launched in 1765.

COOK

1769

The sailors were for the most part pressed men, but there was a notable difference between them and the seamen of Dampier's time. They were, and remained for long after, wild, improvident, overgrown children such as the nautical novelists who wrote a few years later have pictured them; but the lawless rascals who manned king's ships or were pirates by turns, as fortune provided, were rapidly dying out, and veterans of the Spanish main were mostly to be found spending the evening of their days spinning yarns of treasure islands to the yokels of the village alehouse.

One of the causes which led to this improvement in the class of seamen was the disgraceful behaviour of the crew of the *Wager*, a ship of Anson's squadron, when she was lost off the Horn in 1740. A good deal of the trouble was owing to the then state of the law, by which the pay of and control over a ship's company ceased upon her wreck. The law was so amended as to enlist seamen until regularly discharged from the service by the captain of the ship under the orders of the Admiralty.

The food of sailors and the accommodation provided for them were little, if any, better than these things had been fifty years before—for the matter of that than they remained for fifty years later, and to the shame of those responsible, than the food still is in many merchant ships, for even now occasionally we hear of cases of scurvy on shipboard—a disease which Cook, over 120 years ago, avoided, though voyaging in such a manner as nowadays is unknown.

But the most important change that had come to the sea service was in the methods of finding a ship's position at sea. Hadley's sextant was in use in 1731, Harrison's chronometer in 1762, and five years later the first number of the *Nautical Almanac* was published, so that when Cook sailed longitude was no longer found by rule of thumb, and the great navigator, more than any other man, was able to and did, prove the value of these discoveries.

1766-1769

In 1764 Byron, who had been a midshipman on the *Wager*, sailed as commodore of an expedition consisting of two ships, the *Dolphin* and the *Tamar*, to make discoveries in the Southern Hemisphere. This voyage of discovery was the first English scientific expedition since that of the *Roebuck*. Byron returned in 1766 without touching at New Holland, his principal discovery being the Falkland Islands. Three months after his return another expedition sailed under the command of Wallis in the *Dolphin*, and with Carteret in the *Swallow*. The voyage resulted in many minor discoveries, but will be chiefly remembered for that of Tahiti and the story of Wallis' stay there. The *Dolphin* reached England in May, 1768. The two vessels had previously separated in Magellan Straits; and the *Swallow*, pursuing a different course to that taken by the *Dolphin*, made many discoveries, including Pitcairn Island; the Sandwich Group; and several islands in the neighbourhood of New Guinea, New Ireland and the Admiralty Islands. The *Swallow* reached England six months after Cook sailed. The *Dolphin's* return so long before her consort alarmed the Admiralty for the safety of the *Swallow*, and Carteret on his way home, falling in with the French scientific expedition under Bougainville, who himself had been exploring in the Pacific, was informed that two vessels had been sent out to search for him and his men, who, it was thought, might be cast away in the Straits of Magellan.

Dampier's voyage was made solely for discovery purposes; Anson, who forty years later went into the South Seas and so near to Australia as the Philippines, had gone out to fight; Byron, Wallis, and Carteret, who immediately preceded Cook, had sailed to discover and chart new countries; but Cook, who made the greatest discovery and did more important charting than all of them put together, sailed in the *Endeavour* for the purpose of making certain astronomical observations, and exploration was only a secondary object of the voyage. Wallis' return determined the spot where the observations could best be carried out; and, on his advice, Cook was ordered to make for Port Royal, in Tahiti.

One incident in the matter of Cook's appointment should be noted in this connection. The command of the expedition was at first intended for Dalrymple, the celebrated geographer and then chief hydrographer to the Admiralty. The precedent of Halley's command of the *Paramour* in 1698 had taught a lesson of the danger of giving the command of a ship to a landsman, and Sir Edward (afterwards Lord) Hawke, First Lord of the Admiralty in 1768, said, to his everlasting credit, that he would sooner cut off his right hand than sign a commission for any person who had not been bred a seaman. Dalrymple, there is little doubt, never forgave Cook for taking his place, and later on showed his resentment by an unfair statement which will be presently alluded to.

1768

The *Endeavour* was what was then known as a "cat-built" ship, of 368 tons burden, a description of vessel then much used in the Baltic and coal trade, having large carrying capacity, with small draught. A pencil sketch by Buchan (one of the artists who accompanied Cook) of her hull, lying at Deptford, shows the short, stumpy north-country collier, of which even nowadays one may occasionally see specimens afloat. Her great, square stern has a row of four glazed windows, alternated with ornamental panels and surrounded by scroll work, and two square ports underneath them close to the water's edge, probably for loading and unloading Baltic timber. The usual stern-lantern "tops off" the structure. There is a framework for a quarterdeck extending to the waist and the frame of a topgallant poop above this, Buchan probably having made the sketch when she was refitting for the voyage and this structure being erected for the accommodation of the officers.

Cook was appointed a first lieutenant in the navy and commander of the *Endeavour* on May 25th, 1768, and his ship's company, all told, numbered eighty-five persons.

Sir Joseph Banks (then plain Mr.), Green the astronomer, Dr. Solander the naturalist, two draughtsmen, and a staff of servants were also on board. The ship, for defence against savages it is to be presumed, carried ten four-pound carriage guns and twelve swivels. The food supply was for eighteen months, and consisted of beef, pork, peas, oatmeal, butter, cheese, oil, vinegar, beer, and brandy, and included materials for Dr. McBride's method of treating the scurvy. The Admiralty gave Cook a special order on this matter, in which they say:—

> "The malt must be ground under the direction of the surgeon, and made into wort (fresh every day, especially in hot weather) in the following manner viz.: Take one quart of ground malt and pour on it three quarts of boiling water; stir them well, and let the mixture stand close covered up for three or four hours, after which strain off the liquor.
>
> "The wort so prepared is then to be boiled into a panada with sea-biscuit or dried fruits usually carried to sea. The patient must make at least two meals a day on the

said panada, and should drink a quart or more of the fresh infusion, as it may agree with him, every twenty-four hours. The surgeon is to keep an exact journal of the effects of the wort in scorbutic and other putrid diseases not attended with pestilential symptoms, carefully and particularly noting down, previous to its administration, the cases in which it is given, describing the several symptoms, and relating the progress and effects from time to time, which journal is to be transmitted to us at the end of the voyage."

1748-1768

We have a curious illustration of the state of the times in the manner of Cook's treatment by the Viceroy of the Brazils, where, on the way out, he touched to refresh. The Viceroy pretended to believe that the ship was a merchantman, and not a king's ship, and therefore wanted her to comply with certain port regulations which Cook was of opinion did not become the dignity of his commission. In evidence of the *Endeavour* being one of His Majesty's ships, Cook wrote to the Viceroy and, among other things, drew attention to the distinctive uniform of his officers, which is a reminder to us that at this time the dress of naval officers was beginning to assume uniformity. George II. suggested the colours which were adopted by the Admiralty order in 1748, and, from admirals to lieutenants, officers were now dressed in blue coats with white facings, lace collars and cuffs, and gold trimmings. The uniform was continually changing, even up to within the last few years, and nowadays one naval officer has as many different suits of uniform as would have served all the commissioned officers of a line-of-battle ship in his father's time.

When Cook left on this voyage he had, it has been shown, many advantages over Dampier in the matter of nautical instruments, but there is little doubt that he had absolutely no knowledge of the eastern coast of Australia. Dalrymple was the first to suggest that charts, which there is no doubt, did exist in Cook's time, and which do indicate the eastern coast, were known to Cook. Without going into all the evidence rebutting Dalrymple's insinuation, which has been discussed often enough, one fact is worth remembering: Dalrymple, the most learned geographer of the period, published his *Historical Collection of Voyages* in 1770, and in that work he makes no mention of the charts; but, on the contrary, his chart of the Pacific only indicates the coastline on the north and the west of the continent. Cook, who up to the moment of his appointment had been too busy at the practical work of his profession to find or study rare books or search libraries for documents and maps relating to the Pacific, was scarcely likely in 1768 to know what was not known to Dalrymple two years later; and also, be it remembered, Dalrymple was very indignant at being passed over in favour of Cook. It may be taken for granted that beyond such books as Dampier's *Voyage,* De Brosses' volumes, and such charts as the library of the *Endeavour* furnished, old maps afforded no help to Cook in his survey of New Holland. Of the charts Cook says something in his journal. In September, 1770, he writes:—

> "The charts with which I compared such parts of this coast as I visited are bound up with a French work entitled *Histoire des Navigations aux Terres Australes*, which was published in 1756, and I found them tolerably exact."

As to what Cook did in the matter of dry geographical details, if the reader wants them he must go to one or other of the hundred or more books on the subject. In a few words, he sailed between the two main islands of New Zealand, discovering for himself the existence of the straits separating them. He first saw the south-east coast of New Holland at Point Hicks, named by him after his first lieutenant, and now called Cape Everard, in the colony of Victoria; from here he ran north to Botany Bay, where he anchored, took in water and wood, and buried a sailor named Forby Sutherland, who died of consumption and whose name was given to the southern headland of the bay. It is worth noting that in every original document relating to this voyage, save one chart, this bay is called Stingray Bay, after, as Cook himself says, the great number of stingrays caught in it. In one chart, in Cook's own writing, the name Botany Bay is given; but all the *Endeavour* logs call it Stingray Bay, and the name Botany Bay was probably an afterthought.

From here Cook coasted north, marking almost every point and inlet with such accuracy and such minuteness as fully justifies in its particular meaning the statement that Cook discovered and surveyed the whole of the eastern coast of Australia. He then sailed through Torres Straits, proving that New Guinea was a separate island, and thence made his way to Batavia.

Before leaving the coast he landed on August 21st on Possession Island, which lies about a couple of miles off the western shore of the Cape York peninsula, and there formally took possession of the continent, observing the usual ceremony of hoisting the colours and firing a volley. According to Hawkesworth, Cook took possession of the country, and named it New South Wales. There is no evidence whatever of this, and Hawkesworth himself was probably the first person to write the name. In none of the official log-books or other documents does any other name than New Holland occur, and until Flinders suggested the name "Australia," "New Holland" was the generally accepted title of the continent.

Another remarkable mis-statement, which is believed by many, relates to the discovery and naming of Port Jackson, the port of Sydney. On Sunday, May 6th, 1770, Cook's official log contains this entry:—

> "Abrest of an open bay; dist. off the nearest shore, two or three miles. Lat'd. obs., 33 degrees 47.
>
> "At this time (noon) we were between two or three miles distant from the land, and abrest of a bay or harbour, in which there appeared to be a good anchorage, and which I called Port Jackson."

It is still often written that the "open bay" was so named after a seaman by the name of Jackson on board the ship; but Sir George Jackson, who afterwards changed his name to Duckett, was at this time, with Mr. Philip Stephens, joint secretary to the Admiralty. Cook named Port Jackson and Port Stephens after these two officials, and there was no seaman named Jackson on board the *Endeavour*. Cook did not enter Port Jackson, and the discovery of the finest harbour in the world was left for another less well remembered, but no less efficient and zealous, naval officer.

The simple entries in the *Endeavour's* logbooks, to the sailor who reads them, tell far better than the fine writing of Dr. Hawkesworth the difficulties which Cook laboured under on this voyage. For example, His Majesty's ship *Endeavour* was so well found that on April 14th, 1770, Cook has this entry:—

> "The spritsail topsail being wore to rags, it was condemned as unfit for its proper use, and taken to repair the topgall'ntsails, they being so bad as not to be worth the expense of new canvas, but, with the help of this sail, will be made to last some time; also took out one of the ship's tents (50) yards of canvas to repair the jibb that was split on the 1st instant, there being neither new canvas nor twine in the ship to spare for that purpose."

But the most serious trouble was when on the 11th of June the *Endeavour* got ashore on the Barrier Reef. Here is Cook's entry:—

> "Shoal'd the water from 20 to 17 faths., and before the man in the chains could have another cast the ship struck and lay fast on some rocks, upon which we took in all sail, hoisted out the boats, and sounded round the ship, and found that we had got upon the edge of a reef of coral rocks, which lay to the N.W. of us, having in some places round the ship 3 or 4 fathoms, and in others about as many feet; but about 100 feet from her starboard side, she laying with her head to the N.E., were 7, 8, and 10 fathom. Carried out the stream anchor and two hawsers on the starboard bow and the coasting anchor and cable upon the starboard quarters, got down yards and topmasts, and hove taught upon the hawser and cable; but as we had gone ashore about high water, the ship by this time was quite fast. Turned all hands to lighten the ship, and in order to do this we not only started water, but hove overboard guns, iron and stone ballast, casks, hoops, staves, oyl-jars, stores, and whatever was of weight or in the way at coming at heavy articles. All this time the ship made but little water. Being now high water, as we thought, hove a strain upon the stern anchor, as I found the ship must go off that way, if at all, but all we could do was to no purpose, she not being afloat by a foot or more, notwithstanding we had hove overboard 40 or 50-ton weight; but as this was not sufficient, we continued to lighten her by every method we

could think of. By that time she begun to make water as much as two pumps could free. At noon she lay with three streaks heel to starboard. Lat obs'ed, 15 degrees 45 So."

This was off what Cook called Cape Tribulation, and on the two following days these entries appear:—

"Light airs and fine weather, which gave us an opportunity to carry out boath the bowers, the one on the starboard quarter and the other right astern. The spare stream anchor we likewise carried out, and got purchases upon all the cables, and hove taught upon all the 5 anchors. At 4 it was low water, so far as we could judge by the rocks about the ship and part of the shoal being dry, which we had not seen before. The rise and fall of the water did not appear to exceed 3 or 4 feet. As the tide began to rise the leak incresed, which obliged us to set the 3rd pump to work, which we should have done the 4th also could we have made it deliver any water. The ship now righted, and the leak gained on the pumps in such a manner that it became a matter of consideration whether we should heave her off or no in case she floated, for fear of her going down with us in the deep water; but as I thought we should be able to run her ashore, either upon the same shoal or upon the main, in case we could not keep her, I resolved at all risks to heave her off if possible, and accordingly tur'nd as many men to the capstan and windlass as could be spar'd from the pumps, and at 20 minutes past ten hove her afloat and into deep water." (He did not do this without losing his anchors, as he tells us, but) "The pumps gain'd on the leak these 4 hours. Some hands employ'd sowing oakem, wool, etc., into a sail to fother the ship. Weigh'd the coasting anchor and warped out to the S.E., and at 11 got under sail, with a light breeze at E.S.E., and stood in for the land, having a small boat laying upon the point of the shoal, the south point of which at noon bore north, distant one mile.

The pumps gain'd upon the leak this 4 hours. Light airs and clear weather. Standing off the shore in for the main. Got up the main topmast and main-yard. Having got the sail ready for fothering the ship, we put it over under the starboard fore chains, where we suspected she suffer'd most, and soon after the leak decreas'd so much as to be kept clear with one pump with ease. This fortunate circumstance gave new life to everyone on board. Anchor'd in 17 fathom water, 5 leagues from the land, and about 3 miles from the shore."

On the 17th they found a harbour where they hove the ship down and repaired her, when it was found that—

> "One of the holes, which was big enough to have sunk us if we had had eight pumps instead of four, and had been able to keep them incessantly going, was in great measure plugged up by a fragment of the rock, which, after having made the wound, was left sticking in it; so that the water which had at first gained upon our pumps was what came in at the interstices between the stone and the edges of the hole that received it."

Endeavour River, Cape Flattery, Providential Channel, and other names on the chart commemorate the accident; yet after all this trouble Cook continued his survey, sailing safely through the cluster of rocks between New Guinea and the mainland. This passage and the Barrier Reef are probably two of the most dangerous places in the world, and more vessels have been wrecked on that bit of coast between the southern end of the Barrier Reef and the Indian Ocean side of Torres Straits than on any similar stretch of coast-line anywhere.

So far the voyage had been without other disaster than this, but on the way back the *Endeavour* put into Batavia to refresh, and in a letter to the Secretary of the Admiralty, dated the 9th of May, 1771, Cook wrote:—

> "That uninterrupted state of health we have all along enjoyed was, soon after our arrival at Batavia, succeeded by a general sickness, which delayed us there so much that it was the 20th of December before we were able to leave that place. We were fortunate enough to loose but few men at Batavia, but on our passage from thence to the Cape of Good Hope we had twenty-four men died, all, or most of

them, of the bloody flux. This fatal disorder reign'd in the ship with such obstinacy that medicines, however skilfully administered, had not the least effect. I arrived at the Cape on the 14th of March, and quitted it again on the 14th of April, and on the 1st of May arrived at St. Helena, where I joined His Maj.'s ship *Portland*, which I found ready to sail with the convoy";

and on the 12th of July he brought up in the Downs, reporting one more death—that of Lieutenant Hicks.

For his services Cook was promoted a step. His after-life and death need no mention here, and although in both his second and third voyages he touched at New Zealand and Tasmania, his connection with Australia practically ends with the *Endeavour* voyage. But a word or two about the *Endeavour's* officers, taken from documents recently obtained by the New South Wales Government, which perhaps contain some things new to many readers.

In the Record Office, London, there are no fewer than ten logs of Cook's voyage; three of these are anonymous, but six of them are signed by the ship's officers, and one, from circumstantial evidence, is no doubt by Green, the astronomer. The signed logs are by Hicks, Cook's first lieutenant; Forwood, the gunner; and Pickersgill, Clerke, Wilkinson, and Bootie, mates. Hicks, as we have seen, died on the passage home; Forwood, after the *Endeavour's* return, is not heard of again. Pickersgill was promoted to be master on the death of that officer (Robert Molineux) in April, 1771. He had previously served as a midshipman under Wallis in 1766-1788, and he served again under Cook in the *Resolution* as third lieutenant. On the return of Cook from his second voyage, Pickersgill was appointed commander of the *Lion*, and sent to survey Baffin's Bay, but he was relieved of the command early in 1777, and then we lose sight of him. Wilkinson also had served under Wallis, but he died soon after the return of the *Endeavour*, and Bootie died on the way home.

The best-known of these log-writers is Charles Clerke. Though only a youngster, he had seen much service. When the Seven Years' War in 1756 broke out, he was, at fifteen years of age, serving on a man-of-war. He was on the *Bellona* in her celebrated engagement with the *Courageux*, off Vigo, in 1761, and he accompanied Byron in the *Dolphin*, afterwards serving in America, where it is probable

Cook first met him. Consequent on the many deaths, Clerke was made third lieutenant of the *Endeavour* after the ship left Batavia, and Cook, referring to his appointment, wrote to the Admiralty that Clerke was a young man well worthy of the step. He again served with Cook as second lieutenant of the *Resolution*, and in Cook's third voyage he was captain of the *Discovery* and second in command of the expedition. When Cook was killed on February 14th, 1779, he took charge, but only survived his superior until the 22nd of August. He died off the Kamschatka coast, and was buried at the harbour of St. Peter and St. Paul. His shipmates erected a board with an inscription upon it over his grave; and La Pérouse, when in 1787 he visited the spot, caused the board to be replaced by a copper plate, on which the inscription was re-engraved.

In a volume of the *New South Wales Records* is printed for the first time a batch of letters from Clerke to Sir Joseph Banks, and these documents so well depict poor Clerke's cheery disposition, notwithstanding that he was suffering from a fear of the King's Bench, and, what was more serious, the sad disease which ended in his death, that we may be pardoned for reproducing extracts from them. The first was written just before Clerke sailed with Cook on that fatal third voyage as commander of the *Discovery*:—

"DEAR SIR,—I am very sorry to inform you that I am fairly cast away. The damnation Bench of Justices fell out among themselves, upset and fairly frustrated the friendly intentions of Sir Fletcher Norton, &c., wrote a rascally letter, hoping that I would not find any inconvenience from it, and put off the adjournment to Monday se'nnight. Now, you know, this is quite beyond our reach; it seems the whole legends of the Bench do not furnish such another incident. Indeed, there's a fatality attends my every undertaking; those people whom I most honour and esteem, that favour me with the name of friend—to them I become a trouble and burthen. However, though we cannot help misfortunes, we can help deserving them, and I am determined that want of gratitude and attention shall never be an accusation against me; therefore I'm resolved to decamp without beat of drum and, if I can, outsail the Israelites, get to sea, and make every return in my power. I think I had better write to Lord Sandwich to thank him, as I cannot now wait upon him—for my visitations must be very private—and ask him if he has any orders for me. Do tell me what I must do on that head, and if you would have me wait on you ere I depart, &c., &c., and believe me in prosperity or adversity.

"Yours, &c.,

"CHAS. CLERKE."

This is followed by another, written on the evening of the same day, in which he says:—

"I this day received a letter from Lord Sandwich, acquainting me he shall certainly order the *Discovery* to sea very soon, in short giving me to understand that if I cannot leave town by the 10th or 11th instant I must give up all. Now, that completes the wretchedness of my situation. I find the Jews are exasperated and determined to spare no pains to arrest me if they could once catch me out of the rules of the Bench; this, you know, would be striking the finishing stroke. Let me, my good friend, entreat the influence of your friendship here. I shall certainly be cleared the 16th or 18th instant, and shall then be happy."

He got away all right, and on November 23rd, 1776, wrote from the Cape of Good Hope:—

1779

"Here I am hard and fast moor'd alongside my old friend Capt'n Cook, so that our battles with the Israelites cannot now have any ill effects upon our intending attack upon the North Pole. I think I acquainted you from Plymouth, on the 1st of August, that I was getting underway; I then got a good outset with a fresh easterly breeze, and made a very good passage to within a few leagues of this land without any kind of accident befalling us . . . We shall now sail in a very few days, and return to the old trade of exploring, so can only say adieu, adieu, my very good friend. Be assured that, happen what will, it is wholly out of the power of durance of time or length of space in the least to alleviate that sense of gratitude your goodness has inspired; but, indeed, I shall ever endeavour upon all and every occasion to acquit myself," etc.

The next letter is a pathetic farewell to his friend, written on the 17th of August, 1779, five days before the author's death:—

"MY EVER-HONOURED FRIEND,—The disorder I was attacked with in the King's Bench Prison has proved consumptive, with which I have battled with various success, although without one single day's health, since I took leave of you in Burlington Street; it is now so far got the better of me that I am not able to turn myself in my bed, so that my stay in this world must be of very short duration. However, I hope my friends will have no occasion to blush in owning themselves such, for I have most perfectly and justly done my duty to my country as far as my abilities would enable me, for where that has been concerned the attention to my health, which I was most sensible was in the most imminent danger, has never swerved me a single half-mile out of the road of duty; so that I flatter myself I shall leave behind that character that it has ever been my utmost ambition to attain, which is that of an honest and faithful servant to the public whom I had undertaken to serve.

"I have made you the best collections of all kinds of matter I could that have fallen in our way in the course of the voyage; but they are by no means so complete as they would have been had my health enabled me to pay more attention to them. I hope, however, you will find many among them worthy of your attention and acceptance. In my will I have bequeathed you the whole of every kind. There are great abundance, so that you will have ample choice.

"I must beg you to present my warmest and most affectionate compliments to Dr. Solander, and assure him I leave the world replete with the most social ideas for his much-esteemed and ever-respected friendship.

"I must beg leave to recommend to your notice Mr. Will. Ellis, one of the surgeon's mates, who will furnish you with some drawings and accounts of the various birds which will come to your possession. He has been very useful to me in your service in that particular, and is, I believe, a very worthy young man, and, I hope, will prove worthy of any services that may be in your way to confer upon him.

"The two clerks of the two ships, Mr. W. Dewar and Mr. Greg Santham, have, I believe, been very honest servants in their stations, and having by Captain Cook's (and very soon by my death) lost those to whom they looked up to for protection, are, I fear, destitute of friends. If it should be in your power to render them any services, I flatter myself they will be worthy of such attention.

"If I should recollect anything more to say to you, I will trouble my friend Mr. King with it, who is so kind as to be my amanuensis on this occasion. He is my very dear and particular friend, and I will make no apology in recommending him to a share in your friends ship [sic: friendship], as I am perfectly assured of his being deserving of it, as in that also of the worthy doctors.

"Now, my dear and honoured friend, I must bid you a final adieu. May you enjoy many happy years in this world, and in the end attain that fame your indefatigable industry so richly deserves. These are most sincerely the warmest and sincerest wishes of your devoted, affectionate, and departing servant, "CHARLES CLERKE."

It will take nothing from the fame of Cook to call his connection with the discovery of Australia an accident. He himself says that, having circumnavigated New Zealand, "we intended to return home by the Cape of Good Hope or by Cape Horn to determine the question of a southern continent," but the season of the year was against this course, and "we ultimately resolved to return by the East Indies. With this in view, we resolved to steer west till we should fall in with the coast of New Holland, and then follow that coast to the north till we should arrive at its northern extremity."

Having adopted this course and having reached the coast, Cook made the very best use of his time, and surveyed it as probably no other man then living would have done, but that he did so is unquestionably due to the fact that the season did not admit of the old regulation pursuit of explorers—the search for the solution of the southern continent problem.

CHAPTER IV.

ARTHUR PHILLIP, FOUNDER AND FIRST GOVERNOR OF NEW SOUTH WALES.

1779

Captain Cook's "discovery" of New Holland was turned to no account until a generation later, and to Sir Joseph Banks more than to any other man belongs the credit of the suggestion. In 1779 a commission of the House of Commons was appointed to inquire into the question of transportation, then, in consequence of the loss of the American colonies, an important problem needing a speedy solution. At this period, indeed up to a much later time, the English prison administration was notoriously bad. The gaols were crowded and filthy, and there was no discipline; no system governed them other than the system of rascality practised by many of the gaolers.

Mr. Banks (as he then was) gave evidence before the House of Commons, and strongly urged the establishment of a penal colony at Botany Bay, giving his opinion, of course, as the botanist who had accompanied Cook and had seen what prospect there was of establishing a settlement at New Holland. Banks from this time till his death took a keen interest in the New South Wales colonizing scheme, and had much influence for good in the future of the colony. He was a man of independent means, and there is not the slightest reason nor the least evidence to the contrary, to doubt his perfect disinterestedness in all that he did. But when President of the Royal Society the caricaturists and the satirists had little mercy on him, believing him more courtier than scientist. Peter Pindar's

Sir Joseph Banks and the Emperor of Morocco is only one of the many satires of which Banks was the principal victim.

The proposals of one Jean Maria Matra and of Admiral Sir George Young for forming new colonies to take the places of those lost to us in America, with the evidence and subsequent advocacy of Banks, ultimately led to the Government's decision to colonize New South Wales. But it was not until 1786 that that decision was reached, and a year later still when Captain Arthur Phillip was given a commission as captain of the expedition and governor of the new colony.

All that is known of Phillip prior to his appointment is contained in a semi—official account of the expedition called *Phillip's Voyage*, published about a hundred years ago. We are here told that his father was a German teacher of languages who settled in London, his mother the widow of Captain Herbert, of the royal navy, and that young Phillip was born in Bread Street, in the parish of All Hallows, London.

It may be presumed that, by the influence of his mother's connections through her first marriage, he was sent to Greenwich School, and thence into the navy, where he began his career under Captain Michael Everett at the outbreak of war in 1755.

At twenty-three he was serving as a lieutenant in the *Stirling Castle*, and later on, when peace came, after a turn of farming in the New Forest, he volunteered to serve under the Portuguese Government. Leaving the Portuguese service with distinction, he rejoined the English navy in 1778, and the Admiralty at once made him master and commander of the *Basilisk*, fireship, soon afterwards appointing him post captain. He commanded the *Ariadne*, frigate, later on the *Europe*, and was then selected for the command of the first fleet to New South Wales. All the remarkable story of the colonizing expedition does not belong to this chapter on Phillip, but it runs through the lives of the four naval governors.

Lord Sydney, the Home Secretary of the day, selected Phillip, and Lord Howe, then at the head of the Admiralty, expressed this opinion on the appointment:—

> "I cannot say the little knowledge I have of Captain Phillip would have led me to select him for a service of this

complicated nature; but as you are satisfied of his ability, and I conclude he will be taken under your direction, I presume it will not be unreasonable to move the King for having His Majesty's pleasure signified to the Admiralty for these purposes as soon as you see proper, so that no time may be lost in making the requisite preparations for the voyage."

1787

It took a long time to prepare the expedition, and when the fleet sailed from Spithead on May 13th, 1787, the transports had been lying off the Motherbank with their human freight on board for months before; yet, through the neglect of the shore officials, they sailed without clothing for the women prisoners and without enough cartridges to do much more than fill the pouches of the marine guard.

There were eleven sail altogether: the *Sirius*, frigate, the *Supply*, tender, six transports, and three storeships. The frigate was an old East Indiaman, the *Berwick*. She had been lying in Deptford Yard, had been burnt almost to the water's edge not long before, and was patched up for the job. The *Supply* was a brig, a bad sailer, yet better in that respect than the *Sirius*, though much overmasted; she was commanded by Lieutenant Ball.

The expedition was a big affair, and it seems curious enough nowadays that so little interest was taken in it. There were more than a thousand people on board, and one would have thought that if the departure of the convicts did not create excitement, the sailing of the bluejackets and the guard of about 200 marines bound for such an unknown part of the world would have set Portsmouth at any rate in a stir. But the Fitzherbert scandal, the attack on Warren Hastings, and such-like stirring events were then town talk, and at that period there were no special correspondents or, for the matter of that, any newspapers worth mentioning, to work up popular excitement over the event.

GOVERNOR PHILLIP

On the way out the fleet called at Teneriffe, at Rio, and at the Cape to refresh; and Phillip's old friends, the Portuguese, gave him a hearty welcome and much assistance at the Brazils. When the ships reached Botany Bay in January, 1788, the voyage of thirty-six weeks had ended without serious misfortune of any kind. Lieutenant Collins, of the Marines, Judge-Advocate and historian of the expedition, thus sums up the case:—

> "Thus, under the blessing of God, was happily completed in eight months and one week a voyage which, before it was undertaken, the mind hardly dared to contemplate, and on which it was impossible to reflect

without some apprehension as to its termination. This fortunate completion of it, however, afforded, even to ourselves, as much matter of surprise as of general satisfaction; for in the above space of time we had sailed 5021 leagues, had touched at the American and African continents, and had at last rested within a few days' sail of the antipodes of our native country without meeting with any accidents in a fleet of eleven sail, nine of which were merchantmen that had never before sailed in that distant and imperfectly explored ocean. And when it is considered that there was on board a large body of convicts, many of whom were embarked in a very sickly state, we might be deemed peculiarly fortunate that of the whole number of all descriptions of persons coming to form the new settlement only thirty-two had died since their leaving England, among whom were to be included one or two deaths by accidents, although previous to our departure it was generally conjectured that before long we should have been converted into an hospital ship. But it fortunately happened otherwise; and the spirits visible in every eye were to be ascribed to the general joy and satisfaction which immediately took place on finding ourselves arrived at that port which had been so much and so long the theme of our conversation."

To understand fully what Phillip's good management had effected, without going into detail, it may be said at once that no succeeding voyage, in spite of the teachings of experience, was made with such immunity from sickness or mutiny. The second voyage, generally spoken of as that of the second fleet, for example, was so conducted that Judge-Advocate Collins says of it:—

"The appearance of those prisoners who did not require medical assistance was lean and emaciated. Several of these miserable people died in the boats as they were rowing on shore or on the wharf as they were being lifted out of the boats, both the living and the dead exhibiting more horrid spectacles than had ever been witnessed in this country. All this was to be attributed to confinement, and that of the worst species—confinement in a small space and in irons, not put on singly, but many of them chained together. On board the *Scarborough* a plan had been formed to take the ship . . . This necessarily, on that ship, occasioned much future circumspection; but Captain Marshall's humanity considerably lessened the severity which the insurgents might naturally have expected. On board the other ships the masters, who had the entire direction of the prisoners, never suffered them to be at large on deck, and but a few at a time were permitted there. This consequently gave birth to many diseases. It was said that on board the *Neptune* several had died in irons; and what added to the horror of such a circumstance was that their deaths were concealed for the purpose of sharing their allowance of provisions until chance and the offensiveness of a corpse directed a surgeon or someone who had authority in the ship to the spot where it lay."

VIEW OF BOTANY BAY

Phillip's commission made him governor-in-chief, and captain-general over all New South Wales, which then meant from Cape York, in the extreme north of Australia, to the "south cape of Van Diemen's Land," then, of course, supposed to be part of the main continent. He was ordered to land at Botany Bay and there form the settlement, but was given a discretionary power to change the site, if he considered it unsuitable.

1788

Recognizing the unsuitability of Botany Bay, Phillip, before all the ships of the first fleet were arrived, set out in an open boat to explore the coast; and so, sailing northward, entered that bay only mentioned by Cook in the words before quoted, "abrest of an open bay," and by Hawkesworth (writing in the first person as Cook) thus:—

> "At this time" (noon May 6th, 1770) "we were between two and three miles from the land and abrest of a good bay or harbour, in which there appeared to be a good anchorage, and which I called Port Jackson."

Perhaps, when Phillip's boat passed between the north and south heads of Port Jackson, he exclaimed what has so often been repeated since: "What a magnificent harbour!" And so on the 26th January, 1788, Sydney was founded upon the shores of the most beautiful bay in the world.

Phillip's "eye for ground" told him that the shores of Port Jackson were a better site for a settlement than the land near Botany Bay, but he had no sooner landed his people than the need for better soil than Sydney afforded was apparent. Then began a series of land expeditions into the interior, in which, with such poor means as these pioneers possessed, the country was penetrated right to the foot of the Blue Mountains. The first governor, despite the slight foothold he had established at Sydney—little better such a home than the deck of a ship—persistently searched for good land, and before his five years of office had expired agricultural settlement was fairly under way.

On the seaboard, although he was almost without vessels (scarcely a decent open boat could be mustered among the possessions of the colonists), with the boats of the *Sirius* the coast was searched by Phillip in person as well as by his junior officers.

Major Ross, who commanded the Marines, and who was also lieutenant-governor, described the settlement thus:—

> "In the whole world there is not a worse country than what we have yet seen of this. All that is contiguous to us is so very barren and forbidding, that it may with truth be said, 'Here nature is reversed, and if not so, she is nearly worn out'; for almost all the seed we have put in the ground has rotted, and I have no doubt it will, like the wood of this vile country, when burned or rotten turn to sand;"

Captain Tench, one of Ross' officers, wrote:—

1792

> "The country is very wretched and totally incapable of yielding to Great Britain a return for colonising it . . . The dread of perishing by famine stares us in the face. The country contains less resources than any in the known world;"

and the principal surgeon, White, described the colony in these words:—

> "I cannot, without neglect of my duty to my country, refrain from declaring that if a 'favourable picture' has been drawn, it is a 'gross falsehood and a base deception.'"

Yet shortly before Phillip left it, in 1792, Collins says:—

> "In May the settlers were found in general to be doing very well, their farms promising to place them shortly in a state of independence of the public stores in the articles of provisions and grain. Several of the settlers who had farms at or near Parramatta, notwithstanding the extreme drought of the season preceding the sowing of their corn, had such crops that they found themselves enabled to take off from the public store some one, and others two convicts, to assist in preparing their grounds for the next season."

In June, according to the same authority, the ground sown with wheat and prepared for maize was of sufficient area, even if the yield per acre did not exceed that for the previous season, to produce enough grain for a year's consumption.

The last returns relating to agriculture, prepared before Phillip left, show that the total area under cultivation was 1540 acres, and the previous year's returns show that the area had doubled as a result of the year's work. Besides this, considerable progress had been made with public buildings; and the convict population, which by the arrival of more transports had now reached nearly 4000 souls, were slowly but surely settling down as colonists.

SYDNEY COVE

With a thousand people to govern, in the fullest meaning of the word, and a desolate country, absolutely unknown to the exiles, to begin life in, Phillip's work was cut out. But, more than this, the population was chiefly composed of the lowest and worst criminals of England; famine constantly stared the governor in the face, and his command was increased by a second and third fleet of prisoners; storeships, when they were sent, were wrecked; many of Phillip's subordinates did their duty indifferently, often hindered his work, and persistently recommended the home Government to abandon the attempt to colonize. Sum up these difficulties, remember that they were bravely and uncomplainingly overcome, and the character of Phillip's administration can then in some measure be understood.

With the blacks the governor soon made friends, and such moments as Phillip allowed himself for leisure from the care of his own people he chiefly devoted in an endeavour to improve the state of the native race.

As soon as the exiles were landed he married up as many of his male prisoners as could be induced to take wives from the female convicts, offered them inducements to work, and swiftly punished the lazy and incorrigible—severely, say the modern democratic writers, but all the same mildly as punishments went in those days.

When famine was upon the land he shared equally the short commons of the public stores; and when "Government House" gave a dinnerparty, officers took their own bread in their pockets that they might have something to eat.

As time went on he established farms, planned a town of wide, imposing streets (a plan afterwards departed from by his successors, to the everlasting regret of their successors), and introduced a system of land grants which has ever since formed the basis of the colony's land laws, although politicians and lawyers have too long had their say in legislation for Phillip's plans to be any longer recognizable or the existing laws intelligible.[B]

The peculiar fitness of Phillip for the task imposed on him was, there is little doubt, due largely to his naval training, and no naval officer has better justified Lord Palmerston's happily worded and well-deserved compliment to the profession, "Whenever I want a thing well done in a distant part of the world; when I want a man with a good head, a good heart, lots of pluck, and plenty of common-sense, I always send for a captain of the navy."

A captain of a man-of-war then, as now, began at the bottom of the ladder, learning how to do little things, picking up such knowledge of detail as qualified him to teach others, to know what could be done and how it ought to be done. In all professions this rule holds good, but on shipboard men acquire something more. On land a man learns his particular business in the world; at sea

---

B A leader of the Bar in New South Wales, an eminent Q.C. of the highest talent, has publicly declared (and every honest man agrees with him) that the existing land laws are unintelligible to anyone, lawyer or layman.

his ship is a man's world, and on the completeness of the captain's knowledge of how to feed, to clothe, to govern, his people depended then, and in a great measure now depends, the comfort, the lives even, of seamen. So that, being trained in this self-dependence—in the problem of supplying food to men, and in the art of governing them, as well as in the trade of sailorizing—the sea-captain ought to make the best kind of governor for a new and desolate country. If your sea-captain has brains, has a mind, in fact, as well as a training, then he ought to make the ideal king.

Phillip's despatches contain passages that strikingly show his peculiar qualifications in both these respects. His capacity for detail and readiness of resource were continually demonstrated, these qualifications doubtless due to his sea-training; his sound judgment of men and things, his wonderful foresight, which enabled him to predict the great future of the colony and to so govern it as to hold this future ever in view, were qualifications belonging to the *man*, and were such that no professional training could have given.

Barton, in his *History of New South Wales from the Records*, incomparably the best work on the subject, says: "The policy of the Government in his day consisted mainly of finding something to eat." This is true so far as it goes, but Barton himself shows what finding something to eat meant in those days, and Phillip's despatches prove that, although the food question was the practical every-day problem to be grappled with, he, in the midst of the most harassing famine-time, was able to look beyond when he wrote these words: "This country will yet be the most valuable acquisition Great Britain has ever made."

1801-14

In future chapters we shall go more particularly into the early life of the colony and see how the problems that harassed Phillip's administration continued long after he had returned to England; we shall then see how immeasurably the first governor was superior to the men who followed him. And it is only by such comparison that a just estimate of Phillip can be made, for he was a modest, self-contained man, making no complaints in his letters of the difficulties to be encountered, making no boasts of his success in overcoming them. The three sea-captains who in turn followed him did their best to govern well, taking care in their despatches that the causes of their non-success should be duly set forth, but these documents also show that much of their trouble was of their own making. In the case of Phillip, his letters to the Home Office show, and every contemporary writer and modern Australian historian proves, that in no single instance did a lack of any quality of administrative ability in him create a difficulty, and that every problem of the many that during his term of office required solution was solved by his sound common-sense method of grappling with it.

He was wounded by the spear of a black, thrown at him in a misunderstanding, as he himself declared, and he would not allow the native on that account to be punished. This wound, the hard work and never-ending anxiety, seriously injured the governor's health. He applied for leave of absence, and when he left the colony had every intention of returning to continue his work, but his health did not improve enough for this. The Government accepted his resignation with regret, and appointed him to the command of the *Swiftsure*, with a special pension for his services in New South Wales of £500 a year; in 1801 he was promoted Rear-Admiral of the Blue, in 1804 Rear-Admiral of the White, in 1805 Rear-Admiral of the Red, in 1809 Vice-Admiral of the White, and on July 31st, 1810, Vice-Admiral of the Red.

He died at Bath on August 31st, 1814, and was buried in Bathampton Church. For many years those interested in the subject, especially the New South Wales Government, spent much time in searching for his burial-place, which was only discovered by the Vicar of Bathampton, the Rev. Lancelot J. Fish, in December, 1897, after long and persistent research.

Those by whom the services of the silent, hard-working, and self-contained Arthur Phillip are least appreciated are, curiously enough, the Australian colonists; and it was not until early in 1897 that a statue to him was unveiled in Sydney. At this very time, it is sad to reflect, his last resting-place was unknown. Phillip, like Cook, did his work well and truly, and his true memorial is the country of which he was practically the founder.

CHAPTER V.

GOVERNOR HUNTER.

Admiral Phillip's work was, as we have said, the founding of Australia; that of Hunter is mainly important for the service he did under Phillip. From the time he assumed the government of the colony until his return to England, his career showed that, though he had "the heart of a true British sailor," as the old song says, he somewhat lacked the head of a governor.

John Hunter was born at Leith in 1737, his father being a well-known shipmaster sailing out of that port, while his mother was of a good Edinburgh family, one of her brothers having served as provost of that city. Young Hunter made two or three voyages with his father at an age so young that when shipwrecked on the Norwegian coast a peasant woman took him home in her arms, and seeing what a child he was, put him to bed between two of her daughters.

He had an elder brother, William, who gives a most interesting account of himself in vol. xii. of the *Naval Chronicle* (1805). William saw some very remarkable service in his forty-five years at sea in the royal and merchant navies. Both brothers knew and were friendly with Falconer, the sea-poet, and John was shipmate in the *Royal George* with Falconer, who was a townsman of theirs. The brothers supplied many of the particulars of the poet's life, written by Clarke, and the name Falconer in connection with both Hunters often occurs in the *Naval Chronicle*.

1760

After Hunter, senior, was shipwrecked, John was sent to his uncle, a merchant of Lynn, who sent the boy to school, where he became acquainted with Charles Burney, the musician. Dr. Burney wanted to make a musician of him, and Hunter was nothing loth, but the uncle intended the boy for the Church, and sent him to the Aberdeen University. There his thoughts once more turned to the sea, and he was duly entered in the *Grampus* as captain's servant in 1754, which of course means that he was so rated on the books in the fashion of the time. After obtaining his rating as A.B., and then as midshipman, he passed his examination as lieutenant in February, 1760; but it was not until twenty years later, when he was forty-three, that he received his lieutenant's commission, having in the interval served in pretty well every quarter of the globe as midshipman and master's mate. In 1757 he was under Sir Charles Knowles in the expedition against Rochefort; in 1759 he served under Sir Charles Saunders at Quebec; in 1756 he was master of the *Eagle*, Lord Howe's flagship, so skilfully navigating the vessel up the Delaware and Chesapeake and in the defence of Sandy Hook that Lord Howe recommended him for promotion in these words:—

"Mr. John Hunter, from his knowledge and experience in all the branches of his profession, is justly entitled to the character of a distinguished officer."

It was some years, however, before Hunter was given a chance, which came to him when serving in the West Indies, under Sir George Rodney, who appointed him a lieutenant, and the appointment was confirmed by the Admiralty.

In 1782 he was again under Lord Howe as first lieutenant of the *Victory*, and soon after was given the command of the *Marquis de Seignelay*. Then came the Peace of Paris, and Hunter's next appointment was to the *Sirius*. There is very little doubt from a study of the *Naval Chronicle's* biographies and from the letters of Lord Howe that, if that nobleman had had his way, Hunter would have been the first governor of New South Wales, and it is equally likely that, if Hunter had been appointed to the chief command, the history of the expedition would have had to be written very differently, for brave and gallant as he was, he was a man without method.

When Phillip was appointed to govern the colonizing expedition and to command the *Sirius*, Hunter was posted as second captain of the frigate, in order that the ship, when Phillip assumed his shore duties, should be commanded by a post-captain. A few days after the arrival of the fleet Hunter set to work, and in the ship's boats thoroughly surveyed Port Jackson. He was a keen explorer, and besides being one of the party who made the important discovery of the Hawkesbury river, he charted Botany and Broken Bays; and his charts as well as land maps, published in a capital book he wrote giving an account of the settlement, show how well he did the work.[C]

1788

In September, 1788, Hunter sailed from Port Jackson for the Cape of Good Hope, to obtain supplies for the half-starving colony. On the voyage he formed the opinion that New Holland was separated from Van Diemen's Land by a strait, an opinion to be afterwards confirmed in its accuracy by Bass.

The poor old *Sirius* came in for some bad weather on the trip, and a glimpse of Hunter's character is given to us in a letter written home by one of the youngsters (Southwell) under him, who tells us that Hunter, knowing the importance of delivering stores to the half-famished settlers, drove the frigate's crazy old hull along so that—

> "we had a very narrow escape from shipwreck, being driven on that part of the coast called Tasman's Head in thick weather and hard gales of wind, and embay'd, being twelve hours before we got clear, the ship forced to be overpressed with sail, and the hands kept continually at the pumps, and all this time in the most destressing anxiety, being uncertain of our exact situation and doubtful of our tackling holding, which has a very long time been bad, for had a mast gone, or topsail given way, there was nothing to be expected in such boistrous weather but certain death on a coast so inhospitable and unknown. And now to reflect, if we had not reached the port with that seasonable supply, what could have become of this colony? 'Twould have been a

---

[C] *An Historical Journal of the Transactions at Port Jackson, etc., etc.,* by John Hunter, Esq., Post-Captain R.N. (London, 1793.)

most insupportable blow, and thus to observe our manifold misfortunes so attemper'd with the Divine mercy of these occasions seems, methinks, to suggest a comfortable lesson of resignation and trust that there are still good things in store, and 'tis a duty to wait in a moderated spirit of patient expectation for them. 'Tis worthy of remark, the following day (for we cleared this dreaded land about 2 in the morning, being April the 22nd, 1789), on examining the state of the rigging, &c., some articles were so fearfully chafed that a backstay or two actually went away or broke."

CAPTAIN JOHN HUNTER

To face p. 96.

Soon after came the end of the old ship. She had been sent to Norfolk Island, with a large proportion of the settlers at Port Jackson, to relieve the strain on the food supply. The contingent embarked with a marine guard under Major Ross in the *Sirius* and the Government brig *Supply*, and sailed on the 6th of March, 1790. Young Southwell, the signal midshipman stationed at the solitary look-out on the south head of Port Jackson, shall tell the rest of the story:—

1790

"Nothing more of these [the two ships] were seen 'till April the 5th, when the man who takes his station there at daybreak soon came down to inform me a sail was in sight. On going up I saw her coming up with the land, and judged it to be the *Supply*, but was not a little surprised at her returning so soon, and likewise, being alone, my mind fell to foreboding an accident; and on going down to get ready to wait on the gov'r I desired the gunner to notice if the people mustered thick on her decks as she came in under the headland, thinking in my own mind, what I afterwards found, that the *Sirius* was lost. The *Supply* bro't an account that on the 19th of March about noon the *Sirius* had, in course of loading the boats, drifted rather in with the land. On seeing this they of course endeavoured to stand off, but the wind being dead on the shore, and the ship being out of trim and working unusually bad, she in staying—for she would not go about just as she was coming to the wind—tailed the ground with the after-part of her keel, and, with two sends of the vast surf that runs there, was completely thrown on the reef of dangerous rocks called Pt. Ross. They luckily in their last extremity let go both anchors and stopper'd the cables securely, and this, 'tho it failed of the intention of riding her clear, yet caused her to go right stern foremost on the rocks, by which means she lay with her bow opposed to the sea, a most happy circumstance, for had she laid broadside to, which otherwise she would have had a natural tendency to have done, 'tis more than probable she must have overset, gone to pieces, and every soul have perish'd.

"Her bottom bilged immediately, and the masts were as soon cut away, and the gallant ship, upon which hung the hopes of the colony, was now a complete wreck. They [the *Supply*] brought a few of the officers and men hither; the remainder of the ships company, together with Captain Hunter, &c., are left there on acc't of constituting a number adequate to the provision, and partly to save what they possibly can from the wreck. I understand that there are some faint hopes, if favor'd with extraordinary fine weather, to recover most of the provision, for she carried a great quantity there on the part of the reinforcement. The whole of the crew were saved, every exertion being used, and all assistance received from the *Supply* and colonists on shore. The passengers fortunately landed before the accident, and I will just mention to you the method by which the crew were saved. When they found that the ship was ruined and giving way upon the beam right athwart, they made a rope fast to a drift-buoy, which by the surf was driven on shore. By this a stout hawser was convey'd, and those on shore made it fast a good way up a pine-tree. The other end, being on board, was hove taut. On this hawser was placed the heart of a stay (a piece of wood with a hole through it), and to this a grating was slung after the manner of a pair of scales. Two lines were made fast on either side of the heart, one to haul it on shore, the other to haul it on board. On this the shipwreck'd seated themselves, two or more at a time, and thus were dragged on shore thro' a dashing surf, which broke frequently over their heads, keeping them a considerable time under water, some of them coming out of the water half drowned and a good deal bruised. Captn. Hunter was a good deal hurt, and with repeated seas knock'd off the grating, in so much that all the lookers-on feared greatly for his letting go; but he got on shore safe, and his hurts are by no means dangerous. Many private effects were saved, the sea driving them on shore when thrown overboard, but 'twas not always so courteous. Much is lost, and many escaped with nothing more than they stood in."

1792

Hunter and his crew were left at Norfolk Island for many weary months before a vessel could be obtained in which to send them to England, and it was not until the end of the following March—a year after the loss of their ship—that they sailed from Sydney in the *Waaksamheyd*, a small Dutch *snow*.[D]

In this miserable little vessel Hunter made a remarkable voyage home, of which he gives an account in his book. His official letter to the Secretary of the Admiralty, dated Portsmouth, April 23rd, 1792, tells in a few words what sort of a passage could be made to England in those days. He writes:—

> "You will be pleased to inform their lordships that upon my arrival from Norfolk Island at Port Jackson (26th February, 1791) I found that Governor Phillip had contracted with the master of a Dutch *snow*, which had arrived at that port from Batavia with a cargo of provisions purchased there for the use of the settlement, for a passage to England for the remaining officers and company of His Majestie's late ship the *Sirius*, under my command, in consequence of which agreement I was directed to embark, and we sail'd from Port Jackson on the 27th of March, victuall'd for sixteen weeks, and with fifty tons of water on board. We were in all on board 123 people, including those belonging to the vessel . . . We steer'd to the northward, and made New Caledonia 23 April, and passed to the westward of it. As the master did not feel himself qualified to navigate a ship in these unknown seas, he had, upon our leaving Port Jackson, requested my assistance, which he had. In sailing to the northward we fell in with several islands and shoals, the situations of which we determined . . . No ship that I have heard of having sail'd between New Britain and New Ireland since that passage was discovered by Captain Carteret in H.M. sloop *Swallow*, I was the more desirous to take that rout from his having

---

D   A favourite rig of that period. A snow was similar to a brig, except that she carried upon a small spar, just abaft the mainmast, a kind of trysail, then called the spanker.

found two very accessible harbours in New Ireland, where we hoped to get a supply of water . . .

"We passed thro' the Strait of Macassar, and arrived at Batavia on the 27th of September, after a most tedious and destressing passage of twenty-six weeks, during a great part of which time we had been upon a very small ration of provision. We buried on the passage Lieutenant George William Maxwell and one seaman of the *Sirius*, with one belonging to the *snow*. My transactions at Batavia will be fully seen in the narrative. I left that place on the 20th October, and arrived at the Cape on the 17th December, but being unable to reach the proper anchorage, I was on the 20th driven to sea again, with the loss of two anchors and cables. On the 22nd we again reached the bay, with a signal of distress flying, and thro' the exertions of Captain Bligh, who was there in the *Providence*, we were got into safety, and receiv'd anchors and cables from the shore. My people being very sickly, the effects of that destructive place Batavia, their slow progress in recovery detained me at the Cape longer than I intended to have staid. I sailed from Table Bay 18th January, but left five sick behind me; anchored at St. Helena 4th February, to complete our water, left that island the 13th, and arrived here late last night."

On the way home the *Waaksamheyd* got into trouble with the natives of Mindanao, one of the Dutch Archipelago. The rajah of the place would not supply refreshment to the vessel, and her master threatened to fire upon the native canoes, notwithstanding the remonstrances of Hunter. In the course of the dispute the rajah lost his temper and attacked the shipmaster, whose life was saved by Hunter, but the quarrel resulted in a regular engagement between the natives and people on the ship, in which the crew of the *Sirius*, for their own safety, were compelled to take part. The canoes were ultimately driven off, with great loss of life to the people in them, and the Europeans escaped unhurt.

Hunter's experience on this voyage taught him that the proper route home from Australia was not north about, nor *viâ* the Cape of Good Hope, but round the Horn, and he wrote to the Admiralty to that effect, but it was years later before sailors woke up to the fact. At the Cape of Good Hope a number of English shipwrecked sailors were prisoners of the Dutch, and Hunter's spirited remonstrance brought about their release, and for this he was thanked by the Admiralty. A court-martial was duly held, and Hunter and the ship's company honourably acquitted of all blame for the loss of the *Sirius*.

ATTACK ON THE WAAKSAMHEYD

When it became apparent that Phillip's health would not permit him to return to New South Wales, Hunter (in October, 1793), who was serving as a volunteer captain in Lord Howe's flagship, the *Queen Charlotte*, applied for the position of governor of the colony, and four months later he was given the appointment. Lord Howe, who had been his constant patron, thus satisfying his desire to give Hunter an important command, and thereby depriving the sea service of a very able naval officer, neither to the advantage of Hunter nor the colony he was sent to govern.

In the interval between Phillip's departure for England (December, 1792) and Hunter's arrival in the colony on September 7th, 1795, the settlement was governed successively by two lieutenant-governors. These two officers were Major Grose, the commandant of the New South Wales Corps, who ruled until December, 1794, and Captain Paterson, of the same regiment, who had charge until the arrival of Hunter. The New South Wales Corps had such an influence on the lives of these naval governors of Australia that in the next chapter it will be necessary to give a sketch of this remarkable regiment; meanwhile it may be merely mentioned that the commanding officer of the military, during the period of the four New South Wales naval governors, held a commission as lieutenant-governor, and so took command in the absence of the governor.

Upon Hunter's arrival he did not at all like the state of affairs. Major Grose had permitted to grow up a system of trade in which his officers had secured monopolies, and, as a leading article of this commerce was rum, it can easily be understood in what a state of disorder Hunter found the colony. Instead of the prisoners being kept at work cultivating the ground, the officers of the New South Wales Regiment employed more than a proper proportion of them in their private affairs; and the consequence was, the settlement had made little or no progress on the road to independence—that is, of course, independence in the matter of growing its food supply, not its politics. Further than this, Grose's methods of governing a colony and administering its laws were the same as those he employed in commanding his regiment. He was not able to rise above this; and under him martial law was practically, if not nominally, the form of the colony's government. Paterson, his successor, passively carried on until the arrival of Hunter the same lines as his predecessor; and the consequence was, the colony existed for the benefit of the officers of the regiment, who, by huckstering in stores, were rapidly acquiring fortunes. A few free settlers had already arrived in the colony, and by degrees emancipated prisoners and emigrants from Great Britain were forming a small free population, and were beginning to have "interests." Thus there were slowly growing the elements of a pretty quarrel, a triangular duel, in which officials, free emigrants, and emancipated convicts had all interests to serve, and which for many long years after was the constant bugbear of the governor of the colony.

By the time Hunter arrived there were a number of time-expired prisoners in the settlement, and these became an increasing and constant danger. Retreating into the back country, and herding with the blacks, or thieving from the farmers, they merged into what were known later on as bushrangers. From these men and the ill-disciplined and gaol-bird soldiers of the New South Wales Corps the peaceably disposed inhabitants were in much greater danger than they ever were from the aborigines.

But although Hunter's despatches are full of complaints of the soldiers, of the want of stores, and the need of honest, free men to cultivate the soil by way of a leaven to the hundreds of convicts who were arriving every year, he, like Phillip, believed that New South Wales would ultimately become a prosperous colony. More than this, it was under Hunter that Bass and Flinders did most of their surveying; that Shortland discovered Newcastle; and to no governor more than to Hunter is credit due for the interest he took in exploration.

Here is a picture of the colony in the time of Hunter's governorship, painted by certain missionaries who had been driven by the natives of Tahiti from their island, and who had taken refuge in New South Wales:—

> "His Majesty's ship the *Buffalo*, Captain Kent, being on the eve of sailing from the colony for the Cape of Good Hope, we embrace the opportunity of confirming our letter to you of the 1st September, 1798, by the *Barwell*. Here we have to contend with the depravity and corruptions of the human heart heightened and confirmed in all its vicious habits by long and repeated indulgences of inbred corruption, each one following the bent of his own corrupt mind, and countenancing his neighbour in the pursuit of sensual gratifications. Here iniquity abounds, and those outward gross sins which in Europe would render a person contemptible in the public eye, and obnoxious to the civil law, are become fashionable and familiar—adultery, fornication, theft, drunkenness, extortion, violence, and uncleanness of every kind, the natural concomitants of deism and infidelity, which have boldly thrown off the mask, and stalk through the colony in the open face of the sun, so that it is no uncommon thing to hear a person say, 'When I was a Christian, I thought so and so.'"

This is strong, but it is true.

This letter was addressed to the directors of the London Missionary Society, and many of similar purport written by Johnson and Marsden, the chaplains of the settlement, are to be found in the records. All these writers agree on one point: the colony had fallen from grace under the military administration. Phillip had left it in good order, and Hunter at the time, these witnesses testified, was doing his best to improve matters.

Lang (not a reliable authority in many things, but to be believed when not expressing opinions), in his *History of New South Wales*, tells an anecdote of Hunter which is worth retelling. Captain Hunter was on one occasion the subject of an anonymous letter addressed by some disreputable colonist to the Duke of Portland, then Home Secretary. (There was no Colonial Secretary in those days.) The Duke sent back the letter without comment to Hunter, who one day handed it to an officer who was dining with him. "You will surely notice this?" said the officer. "No," replied Hunter. "The man has a family, and I don't want to ruin them."

It was this good-nature, this disinclination to fight his enemies to the bitter end, that ultimately had much to do with Hunter's recall. A certain Captain John MacArthur, of the New South Wales Corps, of whom we shall presently hear very much, was, when Hunter arrived, filling the civil post of Inspector of Public Works. He was also a settler in the full meaning of the word, owning many acres and requiring many assigned servants to work them and to look after his flocks and herds, and from some cause connected with these civil occupations he came into collision with the governor. This presently led to much correspondence between the Home Office, the governor, and MacArthur. In these letters Hunter and his subordinate say very unkind things of each other, which nowadays may well be forgotten. The settlement was so small, the life was such an uneventful one, that it would be wonderful indeed if men did not quarrel, and these two men were naturally antagonistic to each other.

Hunter was an old-fashioned naval officer, sixty years of age, and fifty of those years had been spent in disinterested service to his country, "a pleasant, sensible old man," says a young ship's officer, writing home to his father; and in another letter, published in a newspaper of 1798, we are told that "much may be expected from Captain Hunter, whose virtue and integrity is as conspicuous as his merit."

MacArthur was a comparatively young man, who had come to the colony less with the intention of soldiering than of making himself a home. He was an excellent colonist and a perfectly honourable man, but he was the very worst kind of a subordinate that a man with Hunter's lack of strong personality could have under him. MacArthur wanted to develop the resources of the colony and improve his farm at the same time, and that he had it in him to do these things is proved by after-events. The name of MacArthur, the father of the merino wool industry, is the best-remembered name in Australia today; but poor old Hunter could not recognise the soldier man's merits, and so he added to his legitimate quarrel with the meaner hucksters of his officials the quarrel with the enterprising MacArthur; and, although there is no written evidence to prove it, there is little doubt that MacArthur's letters to England had due effect upon the minds of the home authorities.

The Duke of Portland wrote to Hunter early in 1799 requesting him to afford the fullest refutation of a number of charges that had been made against the administration of the colony. Wrote the Duke:—

> "I proceed to let you know that it is asserted that the price of necessary articles is of late doubled; that the same wheat is received into the Government stores at ten shillings per bushel which the settler is under the necessity of selling to the huckster at three shillings; that spirits or other articles are purchased by the officers of His Majesty's forces in New South Wales, and retailed by them at the most exorbitant prices to the lowest order of the settlers and convicts; that the profit on such articles is often at the rate of one hundred shillings for one; that this sort of traffic is not confined to the officers, but is carried on in the Government House, although it is not affirmed that you have any participation in such proceedings; that the officers and favoured individuals are allowed to send large quantities of grain into the Government stores, whilst those who have only the ability to raise small crops are refused, and consequently are obliged to sell their produce to hucksters at the low rate above mentioned."

Now many of these allegations were true, for Hunter himself had written repeatedly complaining of the existence of such abuses, and had been answered, "Well, put a stop to them." Then he would publish a "Public Order" or some similar document telling the hucksters they were not to do these things; the offenders would go on offending, and Hunter would go on publishing more "Public Orders."

Hunter received the above letter from Portland in November, 1799. Before he could write a reply to it, the Duke wrote him another letter. There were several pages relating to details of administration; but it might have been written by a woman, for the last paragraph contained the all-important part in these words:—

1800

"Having now made all the observations which appear to me to be necessary on the points contained in your several despatches which are now before me, it is with my very sincere concern that I find myself obliged to add that I feel myself called upon by the sense of the duty which I owe to the situation in which I have the honour to be placed to express my disapprobation of the manner in which the government of the settlement has been administered by you in so many respects; that I am commanded to signify you the King's pleasure to return to this kingdom by the first safe conveyance which offers itself after the arrival of Lieutenant-Governor King, who is authorized by His Majesty to take upon him the government of that settlement immediately on your departure from it."

The poor old governor was very indignant. He denounced in strong language the "anonymous assassin" who he thinks accused him to His Grace of conniving at the trading he was endeavouring to suppress.

"Can it be suppos'd, my lord, that a man at my time of life, holding the rank I have the honour to be arriv'd at in the profession I have been bred in, and to which I have risen by virtue of a character never yet stain'd by one mean, base, or dishonourable action—can it be conceived that after having by a life truly and sincerely devoted to the service of my sovereign, after having spent forty-six years of that life in constant and active employment in all the quarters of the world, during which I have risen thro' all the ranks and gradations of my profession and at last arriv'd at the highly flattering and exalted office of being appointed the representative of His Majesty in this remote part of his dominions—can it be believ'd, my lord, that a man possessing a single spark of virtuous principles could be prevailed on thro' any latent object, any avaricious view, by any act so mean, so low, so contemptible, as that of which this anonymous villain has dared to suppose me capable, to bring disgrace upon that elevated situation? No, my lord, I thank God I possess a share of pride sufficient to keep me far above any mean or degrading action. I am satisfied with what the Crown allows me, altho' that, in my situation in this expensive country, is small enough, yet, my lord, I am satisfied, nor do I conceive it consistent with the dignity of my office to endeavour in any way whatever to gain more, were it even in a less censurable manner than that which has been mention'd. Let me live upon bread and water with a pure and unpolluted conscience, a fair and respectable character, in preference to rolling in wealth obtained by such infamous, such shameful, such ignominious means as this letter-writer alludes to."

It is a long while ago since this letter was written by a rough old sailor, and its quaint wording may raise a smile, but Hunter was very much in earnest; and if his failure to govern convicts and "officers and gentlemen" who traded in rum is to count against him, leaving but a contemptuous pity for a weak old man as an impression on the mind, go back to his sea-days, when he fought the crazy old *Sirius* through a hurricane to bring food to these shore-people, and remember him for this closing anecdote of his life:—

1801-1821

In 1801, soon after his arrival in England, Hunter commanded the *Venerable* (74). He was cruising off Torbay, when a man fell overboard. Hunter attempted to put the ship about to pick him up; she missed stays, ran ashore, and became a wreck. At the court-martial (at which Hunter was honourably acquitted) he was asked whether he thought he was justified in putting the ship about in such circumstances, to which question he replied, "I consider the life of a British seaman of more value than any ship in His Majesty's navy."

When he returned to England, he was granted a pension, for his services as governor, of £300 per annum; was promoted rear-admiral in October, 1807, and became vice-admiral of the Red in July, 1810. He died in Judd Street, London, in March, 1821, aged eighty-three, and was buried in Hackney churchyard, where a tombstone with a long inscription records his services.

CHAPTER VI.

THE MARINES AND THE NEW SOUTH WALES CORPS.

The service of the Marines in the colonization of Australia was, as it always has been, *per mare, per terram*, such as reflected the highest credit upon the corps. They were not "Royal" in those days, nor were they light infantry; the first title came to them in 1802, when their facings were changed from white to royal blue, and it was not until 1855 that they were designated light infantry.

The Marine force in the first fleet under Captain Phillip numbered, including women and children, 253 persons, made up of a major commanding, 1 judge-advocate, 2 captains, 2 captain-lieutenants, 9 first lieutenants, 3 second lieutenants, 1 adjutant, 1 quarter-master, 12 sergeants, 12 corporals, 8 drummers, 160 privates, 30 women, and 12 children. The detachment was drawn from the Portsmouth and Plymouth divisions in equal numbers. This expedition to Botany Bay was a service more remote from home than any the corps had before been engaged in, and the men so looked upon it, as may be seen from the following tedious memorial, which one company addressed to the officer commanding:—

> "We, the marines embarked on board the *Scarborough*, who have voluntarily entered on a dangerous expedition, replete with numberless difficulties, which in the faithful discharge of our duty we must necessarily be exposed to, and supposing ourselves to be on the same footing as if embarked on any of His Maj's ships of war, or as the seamen and marines on the same expedition with us—we hope

to receive the same indulgence, now conceive ourselves sorely aggrieved by finding the intentions of Government to make no allowance of spirituous liquor or wine after our arrival at the intended colony in New South Wales. A moderate distribution of the above-mentioned article being indispensibly requisite for the preservation of our lives, which change of climate and the extreme fatigue we shall be necessarily exposed to may probably endanger, we therefore humbly entreat you will be pleased to convey these our sentiments to Major Ross. Presuming, sir, that you will not only be satisfied that our demand is reasonable, but will also perceive the urgent necessity there is for a compliance with our request, we flatter ourselves you will also use your influence to cause a removal of the uneasiness we experience under the idea of being restricted in the supply of one of the principal necessarys of life, without which, for the reasons above stated, we cannot expect to survive the hardships incident to our situation. You may depend on a chearful and ready discharge of the public duties that may be enjoyned on us. The design of Government is, we hope, to have a feeling for the calamities we must encounter. So, as to induce them to provide in a moderate and reasonable degree for our maintenance and preservation, we beg leave to tender our most dutiful assurances of executing to the utmost of our power our several abilities in the duty assign'd, so that we remain in every respect loyal subjects to our king and worthy members of society."

The request was granted, and a three years' supply of spirits was put on board the transports.

1788-1792

Several officers of this force are entitled to be remembered in connection with the founding of New South Wales. Major Ross, the commandant and lieutenant-governor of the colony, was a captain in the Plymouth division when appointed to New South Wales, and was then given the rank of brevet-major. From the day of his arrival in the colony until his return to England he was a constant thorn in the side of the governor. A man more unsuitable for the particular service could not have been chosen. He was a most excellent pipe-clay and stock type of soldier, and his men appear to have been kept well in hand, in spite of a service peculiarly calculated to subvert discipline, but there his qualifications ended.

He conceived that the sole duty of himself and his command was to defend the settlement from foreign invasion and to mount guard over the prisoners. The governor wanted to form a criminal court, as empowered by his commission, and to do this it was necessary to call upon the marine officers to sit upon it. Ross would have nothing to do with it until Phillip, by superior diplomacy, conquered his objections. Ross, in fact, would have it that no civilian duty should be expected of him; and when Phillip forced him to admit that the British Government had sent him out to do more than mount guard, he quoted regulations and many other red-tape reasons why he should not be anything but a soldier. To crown this, he quarrelled with all his subordinate officers in turn, and at one time had them nearly all under arrest together. During his service in the colony he wrote many letters to the home authorities urging the abandonment of the settlement asserting that it was utterly impossible that it could be colonized. He returned to England early in 1792, and the Government showed its appreciation of his value by making a recruiting officer of him, and he died in that service at Ipswich in June, 1794.

There are three other officers whose names are familiar to most Australians: Tench, Collins, and Dawes. The last-named acted as artillery and engineer officer to the colony, and did incalculable service in surveying work. He built an observatory and a battery at the head of Sydney Cove, which, though altered out of recognition, still bears the name of Dawes' Battery. Captain Tench wrote the most readable book giving an account of the settlement, and as about half a dozen books were written by different officers of the first fleet, this, if it is all, is something to be said about him.

Lieutenant Collins is the best-known officer. He wrote an official history, and was associated with the colony's progress for many years after the marines went home. His book is drier reading than that of Tench, but it is the standard authority; and all the history-makers, good and bad, have largely drawn upon him for their materials.

In the memoirs of Holt, the "Irish rebel general," who was transported to Australia, and knew Collins well, appears the following truthful account of him:—

"Colonel David Collins was the eldest son of General Arthur Tooker Collins and Harriet Frazer, of Pack, in the King's County, Ireland, and grandson of Arthur Collins, author of *The Peerage of England*, etc. He was born on the 3rd of March, 1756, and received a liberal education under the Rev. Mr. Marshall, master of the Grammar School at Exeter, where his father resided. In 1770 he was appointed lieutenant of marines, and in 1772 was with the late Admiral McBride when the unfortunate Matilda, Queen of Denmark, was rescued by the energy of the British Government, and conveyed to a place of safety in the King's (her brother's) Hanoverian dominions. On that occasion he commanded the guard that received Her Majesty, and had the honour of kissing her hand. In 1775 he was at the battle of Bunker's Hill, in which the first battalion of marines, to which he belonged, so signally distinguished itself, having its commanding officer, the gallant Major Pitcairne, and a great many officers and men, killed in storming the redoubt, besides a very large proportion wounded. In 1777 he was adjutant of the Chatham division, and in 1784 captain of marines on board the *Courageux*, of 74 guns, commanded by Lord Mulgrave, and participated in the partial action that took place with the enemy's fleet when Lord Howe relieved Gibraltar. Reduced to half-pay at the peace of 1782, he settled at Rochester, in Kent, and was finally appointed Judge-Advocate to the intended settlement at Botany Bay, and in May, 1787, sailed with Governor Phillip, who, moreover, appointed him his secretary, which situation he filled until his return to England in 1797.

"The history of the settlement, which he soon after published, will be read and referred to as a book of authority as long as the colony exists whose name it bears. The appointment of Judge-Advocate, however, eventually proved injurious to his own interests. While absent he had been passed over when it came to his turn to be put on full pay; nor was he permitted to return to England to reclaim his rank in the corps, nor could he ever obtain any effectual redress, but was afterwards compelled to come in as a junior captain of the corps, though with his proper rank in the army. The difference this made in regard to his promotion was that he died a captain instead of a colonel-commandant, his rank in the army being merely brevet. He had the mortification of finding that, after ten years' distinguished service in the infancy of a colony, and to the sacrifice of every real comfort, his only reward had been the loss of many years' rank—a vital injury to an officer: a remark which his wounded feelings wrung from him at the close of the second volume of his history of the settlement, and which appears to have awakened the sympathy of those in power, as he was, almost immediately after its publication, offered the government of the projected settlement in Van Dieman's Land, which he accepted, and sailed once more for that quarter of the globe where he founded his new colony, struggled with great difficulties, which he overcame, and after remaining there eight years, was enjoying the flourishing state his exertions had produced, when he died suddenly, after a few days' confinement from a slight cold, on the 24th March, 1810.

"His person was remarkably handsome, and his manners extremely prepossessing, while to a cultivated understanding and an early fondness for the *belles lettres* he joined the most social disposition.

"He had the goodwill, the good wishes, and the good word of everyone in the settlement. His conduct was exemplary, and his disposition most humane; his treatment of runaway convicts was conciliatory, and even kind. He would go into the forests, among the natives, to allow these poor creatures, the runaways, an opportunity of returning to their former condition; and, half dead with cold and hunger, they would come and drop on their knees before him, imploring pardon for their behaviour. "'Well,' he would say to them, 'now that you have lived in the bush, do you think the change you made was for the better? Are you sorry for what you have done?'

"'Yes, sir.'

"'And will you promise me never to go away again?'

"'Never, sir.'

"'Go to the storekeeper, then,' the benevolent Collins would say, 'and get a suit of slops and your week's rations, and then go to the overseer and attend to your work. I give you my pardon, but remember that I expect you will keep your promise to me.'

"I never heard of any governor or commandant acting in this manner, nor did I ever witness such leniency from any governor."

Of the marines it has already been said they behaved fairly well. Some of them were punished—six, as a matter of fact, were hanged for thieving from the public stores, a crime then of the greatest magnitude—but the crimes committed were by individuals, and offences were very severely punished in those days, even in England. Read what Colonel Cooper King says as to the life of a marine:—

"Some of the marine regimental records are interesting as showing the inner life of the sea, or even land, soldier a hundred years ago. In the tailor's shop in 1755, for example, the idea of an eight hours' working day was not evidently a burning question, for the men worked from 4 a.m. to 8 p.m., with one hour for meals. Again, punishments were severe, as the sentences passed on three deserters in 1766 show; for, while one was shot, the other two were to receive 1000 and 500 lashes respectively. In 1755 two 'private men absent from exercise' were 'to be tyed neck and heels on the Hoe half an hour'; while thirteen years later a sergeant, for taking 'coals and two poles' from the dockyard, was sentenced to 500 lashes, and to be 'drummed out with a halter round his neck,' after, of course, being reduced to the ranks."[E]

1789-1790

Before taking leave of the marines the story of what happened when the *Sirius* was lost at Norfolk Island should be told. Lieutenant King, of the *Sirius*, had been sent to colonize the island

---

[E] *The Story of the British Army*, by Lieutenant-Colonel C. Cooper-King, F.G.S. (Methuen & Co., 1897.)

by Governor Phillip, and was acting as governor of it, but when the *Sirius* went ashore Major Ross thought proper to establish martial law, and so (the quotation is from King's journal)—

> "at 8 a.m. on March 22nd, 1790, every person in the settlement was assembled under the lower flagstaff, where the Union flag was hoisted. The troops were drawn up in two lines, having the Union at their head in the centre, with the colours of the detachment displayed, the *Sirius's* ship's company on the right and the convicts on the left, the officers in the centre, when the proclamation was read declaring the law-martial to be that by which the island was in future to be governed until further orders. The lieutenant-governor addressed the convicts, after which the whole gave three cheers, and then every person, beginning with the lieutenant-governor and Captain Hunter, passed under the Union in token of a promise or oath to submit and be amenable to the law-martial then declared. The convicts and the *Sirius's* ship's company were then sent round to Cascade Bay, where proportions of flour and pork were received from the *Supply* and brought round to the settlement."

In June, 1789, the Home Government determined to form a corps for special service in New South Wales and bring the marines home. Several suggestions had been made to this effect, and offers from more than one officer had been received to raise a regiment. Ultimately an offer by Major Grose was accepted to raise 300 rank and file. The short and ignoble story of this corps can be traced in the records of New South Wales, and Mr. Britton, in his volume of official history, devotes a chapter to an admirable summary of the annals of the regiment.

Grose was the son of Francis Grose, the antiquarian, who died in 1791. Francis the younger entered the army as ensign in the 52nd Regiment in 1775; served in the American War of Independence; fought at Bunker's Hill; was twice wounded; went home on account of his wounds; was promoted to captain; did two years' recruiting; was then promoted a major in the 96th; then raised the New South Wales Regiment; was promoted lieutenant-colonel while serving in the colony where he, as already has been said, acted as governor for two years between the time of Phillip's departure and Hunter's arrival. In 1795, owing to his wounds troubling him, he was compelled to return to England, where he was given a staff appointment, and in 1805 was promoted major-general.

Nicholas Nepean, the senior captain, entered the service in the Plymouth division of the marines, and had served under Admiral Keppel. He left New South Wales after a couple of years' service, and joined the 91st, and was rapidly promoted, until in 1807 he was made brigadier-general and given a command at Cape Breton. He was a brother of Evan Nepean, Under-Secretary at the Home Office at the time of the foundation of the colony; and the Nepean river, the source of Sydney's water supply, to this day reminds Australians of the family connection.

The only other officers worth noting are Captain Paterson, who had been an African traveller, and had written a book on his travels, and Lieutenant MacArthur, whose name has already been mentioned in the chapter on Hunter, and will reappear to some purpose later on. The last thing MacArthur did before leaving England for New South Wales was to fight a duel. The *Morning Post* of December 2nd, 1789, tells how in consequence of a dispute between Mr. Gilbert, the master of the transport *Neptune*, and Lieutenant MacArthur, of the Botany Bay Rangers, the two landed at the old gun wharf near the lines, Plymouth, and, attended by seconds, exchanged shots twice. The seconds then interposed, and the business was settled by MacArthur declaring that Captain Gilbert's conduct was in every respect that of a gentleman and a man of honour, and in the evening he repeated the same expressions on the quarterdeck of the *Neptune* to the satisfaction of all parties. The quarrel originated in the refusal of Gilbert to admit MacArthur to his private mess-table, although he offered the soldier every other accommodation for himself and wife and family. The Government settled the affair by appointing a new master to the *Neptune* and allowing MacArthur to exchange to another transport.

The corps was raised in the fashion of the time. Grose received a letter of service:—

> "Yourself and the three captains now to be appointed by His Majesty will each be required to raise a complete company (viz., three sergeants, three corporals,

two drummers, and sixty-seven private men), in aid of the expenses of which you will be allowed to name the lieutenant and ensign of your respective companies, and to receive from the public three guineas for every recruit approved at the headquarters of the corps by a general or field officer appointed for the purpose."

Grose made what he could by the privilege of nominating and by any difference there was between the price he paid for recruits and the public money he was paid for them; this sort of business was common enough in those days. Later on he received permission to raise two hundred more men, and a second major, who paid £200 for his commission, was appointed. Such men of the old marine force as chose to accept their discharge in New South Wales were allowed that privilege, and were given a land grant to induce them to become settlers, and these men were, on the arrival of the New South Wales Corps, formed into an auxiliary company under the command of Captain-Lieutenant George Johnson, who had been a marine officer in the first fleet, and who, like MacArthur, was later on to make a chapter of history. The regiment at its maximum strength formed ten companies, numbering 886 non-coms, and privates.

It may be interesting to record on what conditions the marines were granted discharges. First they must have served three years (a superfluous condition, seeing that the corps was not relieved until long after three years' service had expired); there was then granted to every non-com. 100 acres and every private 50 acres for ten years, after which they were to pay an annual quit rent of a shilling for every ten acres. A bounty of £3 and a double grant of land was allowed to all men who re-enlisted in the New South Wales Corps, and they were also given the further privilege of a year's clothes, provisions, and seed grain, and one or more assigned convict servants, at the discretion of the governor. The only available return shows that about 50 of the men, a year before the force left the colony, had accepted the offer of discharge and settled at Parramatta and Norfolk Island, then the two principal farming settlements.

The Home Government made no provisions for grants to officers, and as to free emigrants, they were a class in those days so little contemplated that the early governors' instructions merely provided that they were to be given every encouragement short of "subjecting the public to expense." Grants of land equal to that given to non-commissioned officers could be made, and assigned servants allowed, but nothing else.

Any modern emigrant who has seen what a grant of uncleared land in Australia means knows what a poor chance of success the most industrious settler could have on these terms, and the early governors were in despair of getting people settled, since they could not provide settlers with seeds, tools, clothing, or anything else without disobeying the order not to subject the public to expense.

Emancipated convicts, on the other hand, were allowed much the same privileges as discharged marines. Phillip repeatedly wrote to England on this subject, and he, on his own responsibility, on more than one occasion, departed from his instructions, and gave privileges to *bonâ fide* selectors of all classes.

The English Government was perfectly right in the plan laid down. Its object was to encourage those people to go upon the land who were prepared to remain there, and military and civil officials were not likely to become permanent occupants of their land grants. An opportunity, as a matter of fact, was given to them to supply information as to whether or not they wanted to settle. At that time things looked unpromising, and most of them answered, "No." When it became apparent to the Government that there was a desire to settle, further instructions were issued by which officers were allowed to take up land, but the permission was given without providing proper security for permanent occupation or without limiting the area of land grants. From the omission of these provisions many abuses grew up. A scale of fees absurdly small, seeing that fees were not chargeable to military and convict settlers, but only to people who, it might well be supposed, could afford to pay, was also provided by the Government, and regulations for the employment of assigned convicts were drawn up.

In Governor Phillip's time there was no authority to grant officers any land; in Lieutenant-Governor Grose's time there was no limit to the land they might be granted, and as little value was attached to the Crown lands of the colony, lands probably of less value then than any other in the possession of civilized people, Grose's officers, who had to do a great deal of extra civil work, were given land in payment for that work. Much abuse has been heaped upon Grose for his alleged favouring of officers by giving them huge grants of land, but, as a matter of fact, Grose behaved very honourably; and Mac Arthur, who owned more land than any other officer in 1794, had only 250 acres in cultivation, and the grants to other officers never exceeded in any one case 120 acres. If Grose's land policy was bad, he was not to blame, but the trafficking which he permitted to grow up and practically encouraged was a different matter altogether.

Phillip warned the home Government before he left the colony that rum might be a necessity, but it would certainly turn out a great evil. Soon after Grose took command of the colony there arrived an American ship with a cargo of provisions and rum for sale. The American skipper would not sell the provisions without the purchaser also bought the spirits. This was the beginning of the rum traffic; and ships frequently arrived afterwards with stores, and always with quantities of spirits—rum from America and brandy from the Cape. The officers purchased all the spirits, and paid the wages of the convicts who were assigned to them with the liquor; not only this, but they hired extra convict labour, paying for it the same way, and strong drink became the medium of exchange.

All this has been an apparent digression from the history of the New South Wales Corps, but, as will be seen, the subjects are intimately connected. A later governor, who found the colony not so bad as it was at this time, said its population consisted of people who had been, and people who ought to have been, transported. Little wonder then that the New South Wales Corps, enlisted from the lowest classes of the English population, became demoralized. Most of the recruits came from that famous "clink" the Savoy Military Prison. They had little drill or discipline when they were embarked for the colony, and the character of the service they were employed in was the very worst to make good soldiers of them.

In consequence they became a dangerous element in the early life of the colony; there were frequently breaches of discipline, there were cases of downright mutiny, and their career in New South Wales ended in a rebellion. The responsibility for the last crime, however, is with the officers, and not the men. One mutiny was that of the detachment on the *Lady Shore* in 1798.

1798-1807

This ship was on her way out with female prisoners and a few of the better sort of male convicts. The soldiers joined with the seamen and seized the ship, turning those who would not take side with them adrift in the boats. Among these loyal people were some of the male convicts. The boats made their way to Rio Janeiro, whence the people ultimately reached England. Among the "respectable" convicts was one Major Semple, a notorious swindler of the time, who on this occasion behaved well, risking his life for the protection of the ship's officers—from the soldiers who had been put on board to support law and order! (He afterwards settled in the Brazils, and received his pardon from England.) The ship was carried by the mutineers into Monte Video and there given up to the Spaniards, who later, finding the true character of the people on board of her, hanged the ringleader and delivered up others of her crew to the English naval authorities. The female convicts had been carried off by the soldiers, and when the Rev. William Gregory arrived at Monte Video (a prisoner of war taken in the missionary ship *Duff* on her second voyage), he found these women there. They had by their conduct given the Spaniards a curious idea of the morality of Englishwomen.[F] Among the rebellious soldiers were many foreigners, and when the mutineers seized the vessel they announced that they had taken her in the name of the French Republic. They addressed one another as "Citizen" this and "Citizen" that, and behaved generally in the approved manner of those "reformers" of the period who had been inspired by the French revolutionists.

In the chapters on King and Bligh the mutinies of this remarkable regiment form almost the principal episodes, so we may conclude this chapter with what short regimental history the corps possessed.

As the colony grew in population the corps was increased in strength, until, in 1807, it reached a total of 11 companies, numbering 886 non-commissioned officers and men. In 1808 came the Bligh episode, yet to be described. The home Government

---

[F] The *Duff* was captured by the *Bonaparte*, privateer. Among her passengers were several ladies—wives of the missionaries—and at first the citizens of Monte Video classed them with the *Lady Shore's* female passengers.

recalled the corps, and a battalion of the 73rd, 700 strong, was sent out to relieve it. Authority was, however, given to make up the 73rd to the strength of 1000 by taking volunteers from the corps. This was done, and a veteran company was also formed, and the strength of the 73rd then reached a total of 1234 soldiers, of whom something like 500 men originally belonged to the New South Wales Corps. The remainder of the old corps went home, and was placed on the army list as the 102nd Regiment. Before this its official title was the New South Wales Corps, but the newspapers of the day often varied this by calling it the Botany Bay Rangers and similar appropriate names.

1823-1870

The 102nd served at various home stations until 1812, when it was sent to the Bermudas, and in 1814 took part in an expedition against Mosse Island, in America. In 1816 the 102nd became the 100th Regiment; and on the 24th of March, 1818, the regiment was disbanded, and the regiments which were afterwards thus numbered have no connection with it.

The veteran company lasted until 1823, being linked to each regiment of foot that came out to the Australian station. The 73rd was followed by the 46th; then came the 48th, and soon afterwards the New South Wales Veteran Company, as it was called, was abolished. Imperial troops from that time onward garrisoned the Australian colonies until 1870, when they were withdrawn, and their places taken by the permanent artillery regiment, the militia, and the volunteer forces, raised under constitutional government.

CHAPTER VII.

GOVERNOR KING.

For the reason that all the contemporary historians were officers, and their writings little more than official accounts of the colonization of Australia, the personality of the naval governors never stands out from their pages. The German blood in Phillip seems to have made him a peculiarly self-contained man; the respect due to Hunter, as a fine type of the old sea-dog, just saves him from being laughed at in his gubernatorial capacity; King, however, by pure force of character, is more sharply defined. In reading of his work we learn something of the man himself; and of all Phillip's subordinates in the beginning of things Australian, he, and he alone, was the friend of his cold, reserved chief.

Philip Gidley King was twenty years younger than Phillip, and was thirty years of age when he, in 1786, joined the *Sirius* as second lieutenant. In a statement of his services sent by himself to the Admiralty in 1790, he supplied the following particulars:—

> "Served in the East Indies from the year 1770 to 1774 on board His Majesty's sloop and ships *Swallow, Dolphin*, and *Prudent*; in North America in His Majesty's ships *Liverpool, Virginia, Princess*, and *Renown* from the year 1775 to 1779. I was made a lieutenant into the last ship by Mr. Byron November 26th, 1778. On Channel service, Gibraltar, and Lisbon, in His Majesty's sloop and ship *Kite* and *Ariadne* from 1780 to 1783; in the East Indies in His Majesty's ship *Europe* from 1783 to 1785; in New South Wales in His Majesty's ship the *Sirius* from 1786 to 1790. This time

includes the ship being put in commission, and my stay at Norfolk Island to this date. In His Majesty's service twenty years; twelve years a lieutenant."

King had entered the service when he was twelve years of age, and was previously under Phillip in the *Europe*. He was probably the best educated of the officers in the first fleet, and from his knowledge of French there happened an episode which is a matter not only of Australian, but of European, interest.

While the first fleet were lying at anchor in Botany Bay, two strange sail were seen in the offing. That official historian, Tench, of the marines, in a little touch of descriptive ability, which he sometimes displayed, described the incident:—

> "The thoughts of removal" (in search of a better site for a settlement) "banished sleep, so that I rose at the first dawn of the morning. But judge of my surprise on hearing from a sergeant, who ran down almost breathlessly to the cabin where I was dressing, that a ship was seen off the harbour's mouth. At first I only laughed, but knowing the man who spoke to me to be of great veracity, and hearing him repeat his information, I flew upon deck; and I had barely set my foot, when the cry of 'Another sail!' struck on my astonished ear. Confounded by a thousand ideas which arose in my mind in an instant, I sprang upon the baracado, and plainly descried two ships of considerable size standing in for the mouth of the bay. By this time the alarm had become general, and everyone appeared in conjecture. Now they were Dutchmen sent to dispossess us, and the moment after storeships from England with supplies for the settlement. The improbabilities which attended both these conclusions were sunk in the agitation of the moment. It was by Governor Phillip that this mystery was at length unravelled, and the cause of the alarm pronounced to be two French ships, which, it was recollected, were on a voyage of discovery in the Southern Hemisphere. Thus were our doubts cleared up, and our apprehensions banished."

GOVERNOR KING

The two ships were the *Boussole* and the *Astrolabe*, the French expedition under the illstarred La Pérouse. Phillip was at Port Jackson selecting a site for the settlement, and the English ships, before the Frenchmen had swung to their anchors, were on their way round to the new harbour. But certain courtesies were exchanged between the representatives of the two nations, and King was the officer employed to transact business with them. La Pérouse gave him despatches to send home by the returning transports. These letters and the words spoken to and recorded by King ("In short, Mr. Cook has done so much that he has left me nothing to do but admire his work") were the last the world heard from the unfortunate officer, whose fate from that hour till forty years later remained a mystery of the sea.

Norfolk Island was discovered by Cook in October, 1774, and in his one day's stay there he noted its pine-trees and its flax plant. The people at home thought that the flax and the timber of New Zealand might be used for naval purposes, and as Cook's report said that Norfolk Island contained similar products, the colonization of the island as an adjunct to the New South Wales settlements no doubt suggested itself. Phillip was therefore ordered to "send a small establishment thither to secure the same to us and prevent its occupation by any other European power."

LA PÉROUSE

A separate command like this had to be entrusted to a reliable man, and Phillip, though no doubt loth to lose the close-at-hand service of King, yet felt the importance of the work, and so chose him for it. King left for the island on February 15th, 1788, in the *Supply*, taking with him James Cunningham, master's mate; Thomas Jamison, surgeon's mate; Roger Morley, a volunteer adventurer, who had been a master weaver; 2 marines and a seaman from the *Sirius*; and 9 male and 6 female convicts. This complement was to form the little colony. The *Supply*, under Lieutenant Ball, was ordered to return as soon as she had landed the colonists. On the way down, Ball discovered and named Lord Howe Island, and on March 8th the people were landed at their solitary home.

King remained on the island until March, 1790, doing such good work there that not only were the people keeping themselves, but, as we have seen, Phillip sent to him a large proportion of his half-famished settlers from New South Wales, and when King left the population numbered 418, excluding 80 shipwrecked people of the *Sirius*.

1788

As governor of the island, King combined in himself the functions of the criminal and civil courts, and the duties of chaplain. Every Sunday morning, we are told, he caused the people to be assembled for religious service. A man beat the head of an empty cask for a church bell. His punishments for offences then punishable by death were always remarkable for their mildness, as leniency was measured in those days when floggings were reckoned by the hundred lashes.

King left Norfolk Island to go to England with despatches from Phillip. He sailed from Port Jackson in April, 1790, in the *Supply* for Batavia. The brig returned to the colony with such food as she could obtain, and King chartered a small Dutch vessel to convey him to the Cape of Good Hope.

The voyage home was one of the most remarkable ever made. Five days after leaving Batavia the crew, including the master of the vessel and the surgeon, fell ill from the usual cause: "the putrid fever of Batavia." Only four well men were left. King took command of them, put up a tent on deck to escape the contagion, ministered to the sick, buried the seventeen who died, was compelled to go below with his respiratory organs masked by a sponge soaked in vinegar, and through all this navigated the vessel to the Mauritius in a fortnight.

At Port Louis he was offered a passage to France in a French warship, but, fearful that war might have broken out by the time he reached the Channel, and he might thus be delayed in his mission, he refused the offer, and having cleaned and fumigated his ship, he shipped a new crew and sailed for the Cape, which he reached eighteen days later.

At the Cape he found Riou with the wreck of the *Guardian*, he who fell at Copenhagen, and whose epitaph is written in Nelson's despatch, telling how "the good and gallant Captain Riou" fought the *Amazon*. The *Guardian*, loaded with stores for Port Jackson, had struck an iceberg, and her wreck had been navigated in heroic fashion by Riou to the Cape. To the colony her loss was a great misfortune, and King realized that there was so much the greater need for hurry, and two months later he reached England. This was on the 20th of December, eight months from Port Jackson!

1792

At home his superiors quickly recognized that King was a good officer, and Phillip's warm recommendations were acted upon. He was given a commission as lieutenant-governor of Norfolk Island, £250 a year, and the rank of commander. He spent three months in England, married, and sailed again in the *Gorgon*, which was the first warship, unless the *Sirius* and *Supply* and the Frenchmen are counted as such, to visit Sydney.

Phillip went home, Grose took charge at Sydney, and King returned to his island command, which during his absence had been under Major Ross, of the Marines, and martial law. Then began serious trouble. In England, curiously enough, no thought of New Zealand had been taken yet. Some of the masters of transports to New South Wales, who were already beginning to experiment in whaling (whales in plenty had been seen from Dampier's time), had visited the coasts of New Zealand, and King himself was strongly of opinion that a settlement should be attempted there.

The expedition under Vancouver was, in 1792, in New Zealand and Australian waters. Vancouver induced a couple of Maoris to leave their home for the purpose of teaching the colonists how to use the flax plant, promising the natives that they should be returned to New Zealand. The Maoris were despatched by Vancouver in the *Daedalus* to Port Jackson, and Grose sent them on to Norfolk Island. Little was to be learnt from them, and, as a matter of fact, the attempt to grow and use flax never came to anything.

King was very kind to the two natives, who became much attached to him, and he, anxious to carry out the promise of the white man to return them to their homes, did a very imprudent thing. The *Britannia*, a returning storeship, was detained by contrary winds at the island on her way to the East Indies. The wind served for New Zealand. King chartered her to take the two natives home, and himself accompanied them on the passage to the Bay of Islands. King's reasons for the step were—

> "the sacred duty that devolves upon Englishmen of keeping faith with native races, and the desire to see for himself what could be done towards colonizing New Zealand."

These reasons would justify British officers in many circumstances, but they scarcely warranted King in leaving even for the short period of ten days, the time occupied over the transaction, such an awkward command as the government of a penal settlement. The senior officer under King was Lieutenant Abbott, of the New South Wales Corps; and, instead of appointing him to the command of the island in his absence, King left Captain Nepean, of the same regiment, in charge. This officer was at the time about to go to England on sick leave, and King's reason for his selection was that he had no confidence in either Abbott or the subaltern under him. There is plenty of evidence that King was right in his want of confidence in these officers, but the action gave mortal offence to Grose, and King's absence from the command gave Grose his opportunity. But King did worse: Grose was his superior officer, and until Abbott had "got in first" with his grievances King never offered any explanation of his acts to the senior officer, but sent his account of the trip, his reasons for undertaking it and for giving the command to Nepean, directly to the Home Office.

Grose was unjustly severe, was downright offensive over the business; but, to do him justice, he afterwards realized this, and ultimately considerably moderated his behaviour. But there was another and a greater cause of irritation to the lieutenant-governor at Port Jackson, who, be it remembered, was also the officer commanding the New South Wales Regiment: This was the way in which King suppressed a serious military mutiny at Norfolk Island.

Naturally enough, the men of the New South Wales Corps stationed on the little island fraternized with the convicts. The two classes of the population drank and gambled together, and of course quarrelled; then the soldiers and the prisoners' wives became too intimate, and the quarrels between parties grew serious. A time-expired prisoner caught his wife and a soldier together; the aggrieved husband struck the soldier, and the latter complained. The man was fined *20s.*, bound over to keep the peace for twelve months, and allowed by King time to pay the fine. This exasperated the whole military detachment. The idea of an ex-convict striking a soldier who had done him the honour to seduce his wife, and being fined a paltry sovereign, with time to pay!

1794

Then, in January, 1794, a number of freed men and convicts were, by permission of the governor, performing a play; this had been a regular Saturday evening's amusement for some weeks. Just before the performance began a sergeant of the corps entered the theatre and forcibly tried to take a seat that had been allotted to one of the lieutenant-governor's servants. A discharged convict, who was one of the managers of the theatre, remonstrated with the soldier, who replied with a blow. The ex-convict then turned the man out of the building, and the performance began, King entering the theatre when all was quiet, but having his suspicions aroused by the threatening aspect of the soldiers.

At the conclusion of the performance the disturbance was renewed outside, and a number of the soldiers went to the barracks, got their side-arms, and returned to the scene, threatening what they would do. King heard the noise, and rushing out from his house, seized a man who was flourishing his bayonet, and handing him over to the guard, ordered that they should take him to the guard-room.

This was the critical moment. After a second's hesitation King was obeyed, and the soldiers, at the order of Lieutenant Abbott, their officer, retired to the barracks, where they held a meeting, and resolved to free their comrade by force, if he was not released in the morning. King, who had kept his ears open, took counsel with the military and civil officers, and a unanimous decision was arrived at to disarm the detachment.

This could only be effected by stratagem, although it was believed that but a portion of the men were disaffected. All those suspected of complicity were in the morning marched, under one of their officers, to a distant part of the island on the pretence of collecting wild fowl feathers. While they were away, King, with the remainder of the military and civil officers, went to the guard-room and took possession of all the arms. The lieutenant-governor then swore in as a militia 44 marines and seamen settlers, armed them, and all danger was over.

Just as this was completed, the Government schooner arrived from Port Jackson, and King sent ten ringleaders of the mutiny to Sydney for trial, pardoning ten others. The vessel was despatched in a hurry, and King sent a very meagre letter to Grose, leaving a lieutenant of the corps in charge of the guard sent with the mutineers to explain matters.

1797-1800

Grose assembled a court of inquiry, and its finding severely censured King for daring so to disgrace the soldiers as to disarm them. Grose sent an offensive letter with this finding, in which King was ordered to disband his militia, and generally to reverse everything that had been done; and King did exactly as he was ordered to do. At home the Duke of Portland approved of all King's acts, objecting only to his leaving his command to take home the New Zealanders without first getting permission from Grose.

King left Norfolk Island in 1797, and on his arrival in England, tired of civil appointment, set about looking for a ship.

But Sir Joseph Banks, whose disinterested regard for the colony and its affairs had given him considerable influence with the Home Office, procured him a dormant commission as governor of New South Wales, under which he was to act in the event of the death or absence of Hunter. He arrived in the colony early in 1800, bringing with him a despatch recalling Hunter, and it can easily be understood that the ex-governor did not display very good feeling towards his successor, who was sent to replace him in this rough and ready fashion.

The state of the colony at this time has already been described, and although during King's administration many events of colonial importance happened, we have only space for those of more general interest. King displayed great firmness and ability in dealing with the abuses which had grown up owing to the liquor traffic; but the condition of affairs required stronger remedies than it was in his power to apply, so things went on much the same as before, and the details of life then in New South Wales are of little interest to general readers.

King's determination and honesty of purpose earned for him the hatred of the rum traders, and the New South Wales Corps was in such a state that in a despatch, after praising the behaviour of the convicts, he wrote that he wished he could write in the same way of the military, "who," says King, "after just attempting to set their commanding officer and myself at variance and failing, they have ever since been causing nothing but the most vexacious trouble both with their own commandant and myself."

Captain MacArthur had by this time imported his Spanish sheep, and had become the greatest landowner and pastoralist in the colony. MacArthur wanted to go to England, and offered the lot to the Government for £4000. King had the good sense to see the value of the offer, and in a letter to the Home Office advised its acceptance. To this came replies from both the Duke of Portland and the War Office, expressing the strongest disapproval of the idea and stating that it was highly improper that an officer in the service should have become such a big trader. In 1801 MacArthur quarrelled with one of his brother officers, and this led to almost all the officials in the colony quarrelling with one another and to a duel between MacArthur and his commanding officer, Lieutenant-Colonel Paterson, the latter being wounded. King put MacArthur under arrest, and sent him to England for trial with the remark that if he was sent to the colony again it had better be as governor, as he already owned half of it, and it would not be long before he owned the other half.

The Advocate-General of the army, however, sent him back to the colony with a recommendation that the squabble should be dropped.

During King's administration several political prisoners who had been concerned in the 1798 rebellion were sent out; and, by the governor's good offices, these men were given certain indulgences, and generally placed upon a different footing to felons, a distinction that had not been provided for by the Imperial Government. King has had very little credit for this, and because he *did* deal severely with Irish rebels has been put down by many as a cruel man, but the home Government at first sent out prisoners without any history of their crimes, and King was unable to tell the dangerous from the comparatively inoffensive until he had seen how the exiles behaved in the colony. During King's administration there was an open revolt of the convicts. They assembled at a place called Castle Hill, about 20 miles from Sydney, to fight a "battle for liberty." Here is the report of the officer who suppressed the rebellion:—

"*Major Johnston to Lieutenant-Colonel Paterson.*
"HEADQUARTERS, SYDNEY,
"*9th March, 1804.*

1804

"Sir,—I beg leave to acquaint you that about half-past 1 o'clock on Monday morning last I took the command of the detachment marched from headquarters accompanied by Lieutenant Davies, consisting of two officers, two sergeants, and 52 rank and file of the New South Wales Corps, and, by His Excellency Governor King's orders, I proceeded immediately to Parramatta, where we arrived at the dawn of day. I halted at the barracks about 20 minutes to refresh my party, and then marched to Government House, and, agreeable to His Excellency's orders, divided my detachment, giving Lieutenant Davies the command of half and taking Quartermaster Laycock and the other half, with one trooper, myself, having the Governor's instructions to march in pursuit of the rebels, who, in number about 400, were on the summit of the hill. I immediately detached a corporal, with four privates and about six inhabitants, armed with musquets, to take them in flank whilst I proceeded with the rest up the hill, when I found the rebels had marched on for the Hawkesbury, and after a pursuit of about ten miles I got sight of them. I immediately rode forward, attended by the trooper and Mr. Dixon, the Roman Catholic priest, calling to them to halt, that I wished to speak to them. They desired I would come into the middle of them, as their captains were there, which I refused, observing to them that I was within pistol-shot, and it was in their power to kill me, and that their captains must have very little spirit if they would not come forward to speak to me, upon which two persons advanced towards me as their leaders, to whom I represented the impropriety of their conduct, and advised them to surrender, and I would mention them in as favourable terms as possible to the Governor. C. replied they would have death or liberty. Quartermaster Laycock with the detachment just then appearing in sight, I clapped my pistol to J.'s head, whilst the trooper did the same to C.'s and drove them with their swords in their hands to the Quartermaster and the detachment, whom I ordered to advance and charge the main body of the rebels then formed in line. The detachment immediately commenced a well-directed fire, which was but weakly returned, for, the rebel line being soon broken, they ran in all directions. We pursued them a considerable way, and have no doubt but that many of them fell. We have found 12 killed, 6 wounded, and have taken 26 prisoners.

"Any encomiums I could pass on Quartermaster Laycock and the detachment I had the honour to command would fall far short of what their merit entitles them to, and I trust their steady perseverance, after a fatiguing march of upwards of 45 miles, to restore order and tranquillity will make their services acceptable. Return of arms taken from the rebels: 26 muskets, 4 bayonets on poles, 8 reaping-hooks, 2 swords, a fowling-piece, and a pistol."

The revolt seems to have been the result more than anything else of the number of political prisoners which at that time had been transported to the colony and the quantity of liquor available. Certainly King's government was not severe enough to provoke an outbreak. Sir Joseph Banks, writing to him, said:—

> "There is only one part of your conduct as governor which I do not think right; that is your frequent reprieves. I would have justice in the case of those under your command who have already forfeited their lives, and been once admitted to a commutation of punishment, to be certain and inflexible, and no one case on record where mere mercy, which is a deceiving sentiment, should be permitted to move your mind from the inexorable decree of blind justice. Circumstances may often make pardon necessary—I mean those of suspected error in conviction; but mere whimpering soft-heartedness never should be heard."

Dr. Lang published his *History of New South Wales* in 1834; Judge Therry wrote a book of personal reminiscences dating from 1829. Both these writers describe things they knew, and relate stories told to them by men who had come out in the first fleet. Therry and Lang were as opposite as the poles: the first was an Irish barrister and a Roman Catholic; the second was a Scotchman and a Presbyterian minister. The two men are substantially in agreement in the pictures they draw of the colony's early governors and of life as it was in New South Wales down to the twenties.

Lang and Therry both relate anecdotes of King. The stories do not present him in a light to command respect; the official records rather confirm than contradict the stories. Governing a penal colony seems to have had an unhealthy influence upon the sailor governors; Phillip only escaped it.

King, Phillip's right hand, when a lieutenant, makes a voyage to England in fashion heroic; he commands Norfolk Island at a critical time, when no one but a *man* could have controlled its affairs; he is appointed to the supreme command in New South Wales, and before he has been many months in office becomes a laughing-stock.

It is due to the first governor's successors to remember that they had no force behind them. Phillip's marines were soldiers; the

New South Wales Corps were dealers in rum, officers and men were duly licensed to sell it, and every ship that came into the harbour brought it. "In 1802, when I arrived, it was lamentable to behold the drunkenness. It was no uncommon occurrence for men to sit round a bucket of spirits and drink it with quart pots until they were unable to stir from the spot." Thus wrote a surgeon. "It was very provoking to see officers draw goods from the public store to traffic in them for their private gain, which goods were sent out for settlers, who were compelled to deal with the huckster officers, giving them from 50 to 500 per cent, profit and paying them in grain." Thus wrote Holt, the Irish rebel general.

These men are true witnesses, and the extracts among the mildest statements made by any contemporary writer. Yet, be it remembered, the colony was a penal settlement. The prison chronicles of England at this period are not a whit less disgraceful reading; the stone walls of Newgate, in the heart of London, hid scenes no less disgraceful than the stockades of Botany Bay.

But, though the naval governors controlled New South Wales before free emigration had leavened its population, and in consequence are remembered but as gaolers, they were something better than this: their pioneering work should not be forgotten.

During King's administration sea exploration was carried on vigorously (the work of Flinders and Bass will form the subject of the next chapter); settlements were made at Van Diemen's Land in place of Port Phillip, where an attempt to colonize was abandoned, to be successfully carried out later on; the important town of Newcastle was founded; the whale fisheries made a fair start; and several expeditions were conducted into the interior, always to be stopped by the Blue Mountains barrier. Above all, MacArthur, in spite of every discouragement, made a success of his wool-growing, resigned his commission, and returned to the colony, the first of the great pastoralists. King, to his credit, forgot his differences with MacArthur, and lent a willing hand to the colonist. The first newspaper, the *Sydney Gazette*, was published just before King left the colony, and free settlers began to come out in numbers.

The French expedition under Baudin called at Port Jackson to refresh, and certain matters in connection with their visit are worth telling. Two unfortunate incidents occurred: one an accusation against the French officers of selling on shore certain liquor King had given them permission to purchase from a merchantman for the use of their ships' companies; another incident was the manner of hoisting the English ensign on board one of the French ships, which was "dressed" for a holiday. Baudin explained these matters easily enough. The flag was wrongly hoisted by accident, and the accusation for selling liquor was unfounded, and certain officers of the New South Wales Corps who made the statements did not come out of the affair very creditably.

SIR JOSEPH BANKS

But the most noteworthy incident is explained in this extract from a letter dated Sydney, May 9th, 1803, from King to Sir Joseph Banks:—

"Whilst the French ships lay here I was on the most friendly footing with Mons'r Baudin and all his officers. *Entre nous*, he showed me and left with me his journals, in which were contained all his orders from the first idea of his voyage taking place, and also the whole of the drawings made on the voyage. His object was, by his orders, the collection of objects of natural history from this country at large and the geography of Van Diemen's Land. The south and south-west coast, as well as the north-west and north coast, were his particular objects. It does not appear by his orders that he was at all instructed to touch here, which I do not think he intended if not obliged by distress. With all this openness on his part, I could only have general ideas on the nature of their visit to Van Diemen's Land. I communicated it to Mons'r Baudin, who informed me that he knew of no idea that the French had of settling on any part or side of this continent. They had not been gone more than a few hours when a general report was circulated that it had been the conversation of the French officers that Mons'r Baudin had orders to fix on a place for a settlement at Van Diemen's Land, and that the French, on receiving his accounts, were to make an establishment at 'Baie du Nord,' which, you will observe, in D'Entrecasteaux's charts is what we call 'Storm Bay Passage,' and the French 'Canal D'Entrecasteaux.' It seemed one of the French officers had given Colonel Paterson a chart, and described the intended spot."

So King sent for the colonel, and then,

"without losing an instant, a colonial vessel was immediately equipped and provided with as many scientific people as I could put into her, and despatched after Mons'r Baudin. The instruction I gave the midshipman who commanded her was to examine Storm Bay Passage and leave His Majesty's colours flying there with a guard, and that it was my intention to send an establishment there by the *Porpoise*. This order, you will observe, was a blind, and as such was to be communicated to Mons'r Baudin, as my only object was to make him acquainted with the reports I had heard, and to assure him and his masters that the King's claim would not be so easily given up. The midshipman in the *Cumberland* had other private orders not to go to Storm Bay Passage, but to follow the French ships as far as King's Island, and that he was to make the pretext of an easterly wind forcing him into the straits, and as he was enjoined to survey King's Island and Port Phillip, that service he should perform before he went to Storm Bay Passage.

"This had the desired effect. He overtook *Geographe* and *Naturaliste* at King's Island the day the *Naturaliste* parted company with the *Geographe* on the former returning to France, and as an officer of the colony was going passenger in her, the mid. was instructed to give him privately a packet for the Admiralty and Lord Hobart, in which, I believe, was one for you. These letters contained the particulars. The mid. was received by Mons'r Baudin with much kindness. In the latter's answer to me he felt himself rather hurt at the idea that 'had such an intention on his part existed, that he should conceal it.' However, he put it on the most amicable footing, altho' the mid. planted His Majesty's colours close to their tents, and kept them flying during the time the French ships stayed there."

Notwithstanding their first little differences, King and Baudin parted the best of friends, and to an orphan asylum established by King in Sydney, Baudin sent a donation of £50; but King's action in sending the *Cumberland* after him struck the Frenchman in a different light. He wrote to King telling him that if he had wanted to annex Van Diemen's Land he would have made no secret of it, that Tasman anyhow had not discovered it for the benefit of Englishmen only, and that—

"I was well convinced that the arrival of the *Cumberland* had another motive than merely to bring your letter, but I did not think it was for the purpose of hoisting the British flag precisely on the spot where our tents had been pitched a long time previous to her arrival. I frankly confess that I am displeased that such has taken place. That childish ceremony was ridiculous, and has become more so from the manner in which the flag was placed, the head being downwards, and the attitude not very majestic. Having occasion to go on shore that day, I saw for myself what I am telling you. I thought at first it might have been a flag which had served to strain water and then hung out to dry; but seeing an armed man walking about, I was informed of the ceremony which had taken place that morning. I took great care in mentioning it to your captain, but your scientists, with whom he dined, joked about it, and Mr. Petit, of whose cleverness you are aware, made a complete caricature on the event. It is true that the flag sentry was sketched. I tore up the caricature as soon as I saw it, and gave instructions that such was not to be repeated in future."

Towards the latter end of 1803 King grew very tired of the petty annoyances of the officers of the New South Wales Corps, and he wrote home asking that either a commission should be appointed to inquire into the government of the colony, or that he should be permitted to go to England himself and report upon the state of affairs. With the letter he sent home copies of lampoons which he alleged were anonymously written and circulated by officers of the regiment. Here is a sample of one:—

EXTEMPORE ALLEGRO.

"My power to make great
O'er the laws and the state
    Commander-in-Chief I'll assume;
Local rank, I persist,
Is in my own fist:
    To doubt it who dares to presume.

"On Monday keep shop,
In two hours' time stop
    To relax from such kingly fatigue,
To pillage the store
And rob Government more
    Than a host of good thieves—by intrigue.

"For infamous acts from my birth I'd an itch,
   My fate I foretold but too sure;
   Tho' a rope I deserved, which is justly my due,
I shall actually die in a ditch,
     And be damned."

1805

By way of reply, Lord Hobart, then at the Home Office, informed King, that although the Government had the fullest appreciation of the good service he had done, yet the unfortunate differences between himself and the officers would best be ended by relieving him of his command as soon as a successor could be chosen. The successor, in the person of Bligh, was chosen in July, 1805, and King a few months later returned to England.

In Hobart's letter to King informing him of the decision to recall him, the former refers not only to the unfortunate difference "between you and the military officers," but to the fact that these disputes "have extended to the commander of H.M.S. *Glatton*." Highly indignant, King replied to this in the following paragraph of a despatch dated August 14th, 1804:—

> "In what relates to the commander of His Majesty's ship *Glatton*, had I, on his repeated demands, committed myself, by the most flagrant abuse of the authority delegated to me, by giving him a free pardon for a female convict for life, who had never landed from the *Glatton*, to enable her to cohabit with him on his passage home, I might, in that case, have avoided much of his insults here and his calumnious invective in England; but after refusing, as my bounden duty required, to comply to his unwarrantable demands, which, if granted, must have very justly drawn on me your lordship's censure and displeasure, with the merited reproach of those deserving objects to whom that last mark of His Majesty's mercy is so cautiously extended, from thatperiod, my lord, the correspondence will evidently show no artifice or means on his part were unused to insult not only myself as governor of this colony, but the military and almost every other officer of the colony."

There is, of course, another side to this. Captain Colnett, of the *Glatton*, asked for the woman's pardon on the ground that she had supplied him with information which enabled him to anticipate a mutiny of the convicts on the passage out. On the return of the *Glatton* to England, the *St. James Chronicle* informs its readers that at a dinner at Walmer Castle Colnett dined with William Pitt. Perhaps over their wine the two discussed Governor King, and hence perhaps Hobart's letter of recall.

1808

During King's period of office there were, besides the Irish rebels, many prisoners whose names are famous, or infamous, in story. Pickpocket George Barrington, who came out in Governor Phillip's time, once the Beau Brummel of his branch of rascality, had settled down into a respectable settler, and was in King's government, superintendent of convicts, at £50 a year wages. Sir Henry Browne Hayes, at one time sheriff of Cork city, was sent out for life in King's time for abducting a rich Quaker girl; he was pardoned, and returned to England in 1812, leaving behind him a fine residence which he had built for himself, and which is still one of the beauty spots at the entrance of Sydney harbour.

Margarot, one of the "Scotch martyrs," also fell foul of King, who sent him to Hobart for seditious practices. The governor seems to have punished Scotch and Irish pretty impartially, for Hayes and Margarot were coupled together as disturbing characters and both sent away.

The "martyrs," it will perhaps be remembered, were Muir, Palmer, Skirving, Gerald, and Margarot, transported at Edinburgh for libelling the Government in August, 1793, and most harshly dealt with, as everyone nowadays admits.

King was a Cornishman, a native of Launceston. When he went home in 1790 he married a Miss Coombes, of Bedford. By this lady he had several children. The eldest of them, born at Norfolk Island in 1791, he named Phillip Parker, after his old chief. This youngster was sent into the navy to follow his father's footsteps, and in a later chapter of this book he will be heard of again.

The ex-governor wrote in September, 1808, a letter from Bath.

"As this letter may probably reach you before you sail, I just write to say that I came here on Tuesday with Mr. Etheridge, on his return to London, merely to see Admiral Phillip, whom I found much better than I possibly could expect from the reports I had heard, although he is quite a cripple, having lost the entire use of his right side, though his intellects are very good, and his spirits are as they always were."

This letter was to the boy Phillip, then a year-old sailor, on the eve of his departure on a cruise in the Channel. Seven days later the writer had slipped his moorings, and years earlier than his old comrade had "gone before to that unknown and silent shore."

CHAPTER VIII.

BASS AND FLINDERS

The details of Australian sea exploration are beyond the scope of this work, but in a future chapter some reference will be made to the marvellous quantity and splendid quality of naval surveying in Australian waters.

The story of Flinders and Bass, of the work they performed, and the strange, sad ending to their lives is worth a book, much more the small space we can devote to it. Much has been written about these two men, but the best work on the subject, that written by Flinders himself, has now become a rare book, to be found only in a few public libraries, and too expensive for any but well-to-do book-lovers to have upon their shelves. The printing in New South Wales by the local Government of the records of the colony has led to the discovery of a quantity of interesting material never before published, and in this there is much relating to Flinders and Bass—so much, in fact, that the work of the two men could be described from contemporary letters and despatches, material, if not new to everyone, certainly known to very few.

The dry technicalities of the surveying work, interesting enough to the people of those places on the coasts of Australia which are now flourishing seaports, but where not a century ago Bass and Flinders landed for the first time, are too local in their interests to warrant more than a passing reference here. The bold explorers met with so many stirring adventures that the present writers can only "reel off the yarn," and let lovers of topography go, if they are so inclined, to the charts, and study how much valuable map-making, as well as exciting incident, these young men crowded into their lives.

When Hunter returned to New South Wales in the *Reliance* to take office as governor, he brought with him Matthew Flinders as second lieutenant; and to Sir Joseph Banks, whose influence secured the appointment, this is only one of the many debts of gratitude owed by New South Wales for his foresight and honesty in making such selections. Flinders was then twenty-one years of age. His father was a surgeon at Donington, a village in Lincolnshire.

GEORGE BASS

Robinson Crusoe, so he himself tells us, sent him to sea, and his departure from home was soon followed by that of his brother Samuel. Matthew served first in the *Scipio* under Pasley; then he accompanied Bligh in the *Providence* to Tahiti, and thence to the West Indies (this was Bligh's successful bread-fruit voyage); then he was in the *Bellerophon*, and was present at Lord Howe's victory, "the glorious 1st of June." Two months later he left in the *Reliance* for Sydney.

The surgeon of the *Reliance* was George Bass. From his boyhood Bass wanted to be a sailor, but was apprenticed, sorely against his will, to a Boston apothecary. His father was a farmer at Sleaford, in Lincolnshire; but his mother was early left a widow. The lad served his apprenticeship, duly walked the hospitals, and his mother spent most of her small substance in starting him in business as a village apothecary in his native county. Then, like so many before and since his time, unable to overcome his first infatuation, he threw all his shore affairs to the wind and obtained an appointment to the *Reliance*.

Governor Hunter, it will be remembered, took a keen interest in the exploration of Australia, and he had for some time suspected the existence of a strait between Van Diemen's Land and the main continent. Full of desire for adventure and tired of the routine life of a penal settlement, Flinders and Bass, soon after they landed in the colony, found a new occupation in the pursuit of fresh discoveries, and Hunter willingly lent them such poor equipment as the limited resources of the colony afforded.

A month after the arrival of the *Reliance* at Sydney the two friends set to work, and in an eight-foot boat, which they appropriately named the *Tom Thumb*, went poking in and out along the coast-line, making discoveries of the greatest local value. Then began work destined to be of world-wide importance.

Take the map of Tasmania and look at a group of islands at its north-east corner; they are in what was later on to be called Bass' Straits. Among them are two named Preservation and Clarke Islands; these and Armstrong Channel commemorate the wreck of the *Sydney Cove*, which occurred on February 9th, 1797. The *Sydney Cove* was an East Indiaman bound from Bengal to Sydney; she sprang a leak, was with difficulty navigated to the spot named Preservation Island, and there beached.

MATTHEW FLINDERS

The crew, many of whom were Lascars, were saved, with a few stores. Then the long-boat, with the mate, supercargo, three European seamen, and a dozen Lascars, was despatched in an endeavour to reach Port Jackson, the only occupied part of the great continent, and bring succour to their starving shipmates. They set out on the 28th February, were driven ashore; their boat was battered to pieces on the rocks, and they escaped only with their lives. This happened on the 1st of March, the scene of this second misfortune being a little distance to the north of Cape Howe, 300 miles from Sydney. These castaways were the first white men to land in what is now the colony of Victoria. (The spot where the boat was lost is just over the border.) After resting the men then all set out to march along the coast to Sydney.

Sixty days later three exhausted creatures reached Wattamolla harbour, near what is now the National Park of New South Wales, about 18 miles south of Sydney. The remainder of the castaways had dropped and died of exhaustion on the march, or had been speared by the blacks. Those who survived had purchased their lives from the savages with shreds of cloth and buttons from their ragged clothing, and had kept themselves alive with such shell-fish as they could find upon the beaches. At Wattamolla they had halted to cook a scanty meal of shell-fish, and the smoke of their fire revealed their presence to a fishing boat from the settlement at Port Jackson. The fire by which this cooking was done was made from coal found on the beach there; so reported brave Clarke, the supercargo of the *Sydney Cove*, who found it.

As soon as Hunter heard of the discovery he determined to examine the place. In a despatch home he says:—

> "So I have lately sent a boat to that part of the coast, in which went Mr. Bass, surgeon of the *Reliance*. He was fortunate in discovering the place, and informed me he found a stratum six feet deep in the face of a steep cliff, which was traced for eight miles in length; but this was not the only coal they discovered, for it was seen in various places."

The place was named Coalcliff, and this was the first discovery of the great southern coalfields of New South Wales. Hunter, writing to the Duke of Portland under date of March 1st, 1798, shall tell the next incident of Bass' career:—

1798

> "The tedious repairs which His Majesty's ship *Reliance* necessarily required before she could be put in a condition for again going to sea having given an opportunity to Mr. George Bass, her surgeon, a young man of a well-informed mind and an active disposition, to offer himself to be employed in any way in which he could contribute to the

benefit of the public service, I inquired of him in what way he was desirous of exerting himself, and he informed me nothing could gratify him more effectually than my allowing him the use of a good boat and permitting him to man her with volunteers from the King's ships. I accordingly furnished him with an excellent whale-boat, well fitted, victualled, and manned to his wish, for the purpose of examining along the coast to the southward of this port, as far as he could with safety and convenience go. His perseverance against adverse winds and almost incessant bad weather led him as far south as the latitude of 40°00 S., or a distance from this port, taking the bendings of the coast, of more than 600 miles." (This, remember, was accomplished in a whale-boat.) "He coasted the greatest part of the way, and sedulously examined every inlet along the shore, which does not in these parts afford a single harbour fit to admit even a small vessel, except a bay in latitude 35°06, called Jarvis' Bay, and which was so named by one of the transport ships, bound here, who entered it, and is the same called by Captain Cook Longnose Bay. He explored every accessible place until he came as far as the sourthermost [sic: southernmost] parts of this coast seen by Captain Cook, and from thence until he reached the northernmost land seen by Captain Furneaux, beyond which he went westward about 60 miles, where the coast falls away in a west-northwest direction. Here he found an open ocean westward, and by the mountainous sea which rolled in from that quarter, and no land discoverable in that direction, we have much reason to conclude that there is an open strait through, between the latitude of 39 and 40'12 S., a circumstance which, from many observations made upon tides and currents thereabouts, I had long conjectured.

"It will appear by this discovery that the northermost [sic: northernmost] land seen by Captain Furneaux is the southernmost extremity of this coast, and lays in latitude 39.00 S. At the western extremity of Mr. Bass' coasting voyage he found a very good harbour; but, unfortunately, the want of provision induced him to return sooner than he wished and intended, and on passing a small island laying off the coast he discovered a smoke, and supposed it to have been made by some natives, with whom he wished to have an opportunity of conversing. On approaching the shore he found the men were white, and had some clothing on, and when he came near he observed two of them take to the water and swim off. They proved to be seven of a gang of fourteen convicts who escaped from hence in a boat on the 2nd of October last, and who had been treacherously left on this desolate island by the other seven, who returned northward. The boat, it seems, was too small for their whole number, and when they arrived at Broken Bay they boarded another boat [lying] in the Hawkesbury with fifty-six bushels of wheat on board; then they went off with her to the northward, leaving their old boat on shore.

"These poor distressed wretches" (the seven convicts discovered by Bass), "who were chiefly Irish, would have endeavoured to travel northward and thrown themselves upon His Majesty's mercy, but were not able to get from this miserable island to the mainland. Mr. Bass' boat was too small to accommodate them with a passage, and, as his provision was nearly expended, he could only help them to the mainland, where he furnished them with a musket and ammunition and a pocket compass, with lines and fish-hooks. Two of the seven were very ill, and those he took into his boat, and shared his provisions with the other five, giving them the best directions in his power how to proceed, the distance" (to Sydney) "being not less than five hundred miles. He recommended them to keep along the coast the better to enable them to get food. Indeed, the difficulties of the country and the possibility of meeting hostile natives are considerations which will occasion doubts of their ever being able to reach us.

"When they parted with Mr. Bass and his crew, who gave them what cloaths they could spare, some tears were shed on both sides. The whale-boat arrived in this port after an absence of twelve weeks, and Mr. Bass delivered to me his observations on this adventur'g expedition. I find he made several excursions into the interior of the country wherever he had an opportunity. It will be sufficient to say that he found in general a barren, unpromising country, with very few exceptions; and, were it even better, the want of harbours would render it less valuable.

"Whilst this whale-boat was absent I had occasion to send the colonial schooner to the southward to take on board the remaining property saved from the wreck of the ship *Sydney Cove*, and to take the crew from the island she had been cast upon. I sent in the schooner Lieutenant Flinders, of the *Reliance* (a young man well qualified), in order to give him an opportunity of making what observations he could amongst those islands; and the discoverys which was made there by him and Mr. Hamilton, the master of the wrecked ship, shall be annexed to those of Mr. Bass in one chart and forwarded to your Grace herewith, by which I presume it will appear that the land called Van Dieman's, and generally supposed to be the southern promontory of this country, is a group of islands separated from its southern coast by a strait, which it is probable may not be of narrow limits, but may perhaps be divided into two or more channels by the islands near that on which the ship *Sydney Cove* was wrecked."

The exploring cruise in a whale-boat had lasted from December 3rd, 1797, to February 25th, 1798, and we have before us a log kept by Bass of the voyage. Bass describes in detail all that Hunter tells in his despatch, but the intrepid explorer scarcely mentions the hardships and dangers with which he met. Incidentally he tells how the boat leaked, what heavy seas were often successfully encountered, and how "we collected and salted for food on our homeward voyage stormy petrels" and like luxuries.

1799

Flinders meanwhile, as Hunter says in his despatch, had been sent in the colonial schooner *Francis* to bring back the castaways from the *Sydney Cove*, who remained anxiously waiting for succour on Preservation Island. On the way down the young lieutenant discovered and named many islands and headlands—the Kent group, the Furneaux group, and Green Cape are only a few names, to wit—and he came back fully convinced that the set of the tide west "indicated a deep inlet or passage through the Indian Ocean." He had no time on this trip to make surveys, but on his return to Sydney he found that George Bass had just come in in his whale-boat with his report. Hunter and the two young men agreed that the existence of the strait was certain, and that the next thing to do was to sail through it.

The colonial sloop *Norfolk*, built at Norfolk Island, a few months before, to carry despatches, was selected for the service. She was very small, only 25 tons burden. Flinders was given the command, and Bass was sent with him. The sloop was accompanied by a snow called the *Nautilus*, which was bound to the Furneaux group on a sealing expedition. The voyage lasted from October 7th, 1798, till January 12th, 1799, and in that period the explorers circumnavigated Van Diemen's Land, making so many discoveries and naming so many places, that a mere mention of them would fill a chapter. At the end of his log, Flinders tells us that on arrival at Port Jackson—

> "to the strait which had now been the great object of research, and whose discovery was now completed, Governor Hunter, at my recommendation, gave the name of Bass' Straits. This was no more than a just tribute to my worthy friend and companion for the extensive dangers and fatigues he had undergone in first entering it in the whale-boat, and to the correct judgment he had formed from various indications of the existence of a wide opening between Van Dieman's Land and New South Wales."

Six months later the *Norfolk*, with Flinders on board, sailed along the north coast, making many discoveries, but missing the important rivers. Then he returned to England in the *Reliance*. His tried comrade and friend, Bass, had already left the colony when the *Norfolk* entered Sydney Heads, and *his* after-adventures and still mysterious fate, so far as can be conjectured, are told in what follows.

A company was floated in England to carry stores to Port Jackson on the outward trip, and load for return at the islands in the Pacific or such ports as could be entered on the South American coast. A ship called the *Venus* was purchased for the purpose, and

Bass and his father-in-law (he had just married) and their relations held the principal shares in her. The ship was under the command of one Charles Bishop; but Bass sailed in her as managing owner and supercargo.

The *Venus* arrived safely at Sydney, and Bass made a contract with the authorities to bring a cargo of pork from Tahiti. On his return from this voyage another contract was concluded between him and Governor King to continue in this trade. Meanwhile Bishop, the master of the vessel, had fallen ill, and Bass took command; and the following letter, dated Sydney, February 3rd, 1803, and written to Captain Waterhouse, his brother-in-law, in England, was the last news his friends ever heard from Bass:—

> "I have written to you thrice since my arrival from the South Sea Islands. In a few hours I shall sail again on another pork voyage, but it combines circumstances of a different nature also.
>
> "From this place I go to New Zealand to pick up something more from the wreck of the old *Endeavour* in Dusky Bay, then visit some of the islands lying south of it in search of seals and fish. The former, should they be found, are intended to furnish a cargo to England immediately on my return from this trip; the fish are to answer a proposal I have made to Government to establish a fishery, on condition of receiving an exclusive privilege of the south part of New Zealand and of its neighbouring isles, which privilege is at once to be granted to me. The fishery is not to be set in motion till my return to old England, when I mean to seize upon my dear Bess, bring her out here, and make a *poissarde* of her, where she cannot fail to find plenty of use for her tongue.
>
> "We have, I assure you, great plans in our heads; but, like the basket of eggs, all depends upon the success of the voyage I am now upon.
>
> "In the course of it I intend to visit the coast of Chili in search of provisions for the use of His Brit. Majesty's colony; and, that they may not in that part of the world mistake me for a contrabandist, I go provided with a very diplomatic-looking certificate from the governor here, stating the service upon which I am employed, requesting

aid and protection in obtaining the food wanted. And God grant you may fully succeed, says your warm heart, in so benevolent an object; and thus also say I. Amen, say many others of my friends . . . Speak not of So. America, where you may hear I am digging gold, to anyone out of your family, for there is treason in the very name . . . Pleasing prospects surround us, which time must give into our hands. There are apparent openings for good doings, none of which are likely to be tried for till after my return and dissolution of partnership with Bishop, a point fully fixed upon. With kind love to Mrs. W. and all your family, I am, even at this distance and at this length of time, and under all my sad labours, as much as when I saw you."

1817

At this time Bass was a young man of thirty-four, "six feet high, dark complexion, wears spectacles, very penetrating countenance," says his father-in-law. Nothing more was heard of the *Venus* or her crew until there arose a rumour that the ship had been taken by the Spaniards on the coast of Peru. A Captain Campbell, master of the *Harrington*, is alleged to have made the statement that a Spanish gentleman told him that Bass had been seized when landing from his boat and carried to the mines, and that the ship was afterwards taken and the crew sent to share the fate of their chief. The cause of this seizure was, says one unauthenticated account, because Bass requested permission to trade, was refused, and then threatened to bombard the town.

Lieutenant Fitzmaurice was at Valparaiso in 1803, and he states that all British prisoners in Chili and Peru had been released, and that he had heard of Mr. Bass being in Lima five or six years before. A letter in the Record Office, London, dated Liverpool, New South Wales, December 15th, 1817, says:—

> "I have just heard a report that Mr. Bass is alive yet in South America. A capt'n of a vessel belonging to this port, trading among the islands to the east, fell in with a whaler, and the capt'n informed him he had seen such a person, and described the person of Mr. Bass. The capt'n, knowing Mr. Bass well, is of a belief that, [from] the description that

the master of the whaler gives of him, it's certainly Mr. Bass, being a doctor, too, which is still a stronger reason. I am, etc., THOS. MOORE."

And so in this sad fashion, his fate a mystery, perhaps the victim of savages on some lonely Pacific island, perhaps dragging his life out a broken-hearted prisoner in the mines of Peru, the gallant young explorer passes out of history.

1800

When Flinders returned to England he found an enthusiastic admirer and a powerful friend in Sir Joseph Banks. The young lieutenant was getting ready for publication a small book describing the circumnavigation of Van Diemen's Land, and while he was doing this Banks induced the Admiralty to prepare H.M.S. *Investigator* for surveying service in Australian waters and give Flinders charge of her, with the rank of commander. Banks had everything to do with the arrangements for the expedition; and how much was thought of his capacity for this work is shown by a memo from the Secretary to the Admiralty in reply to a request from the naturalist:—

"Any proposal you may make will be approved; the whole is left entirely to your decision."

The *Investigator*, formerly the *Xenophon*, was a sloop of war, and was fitted out in a most elaborate fashion for the cruise, carrying with her an artist (Westall), a botanist (Brown), an astronomer (Crossley), and several other scientists.

Among her officers were Samuel Flinders, second lieutenant and brother of Matthew, and a midshipman named John Franklin, afterwards Sir John Franklin, the Arctic explorer and at one time governor of Tasmania. Her total complement numbered 83 hands. The *Lady Nelson*, a colonial government brig, was ordered, on the arrival of the *Investigator* at Port Jackson, to join the expedition and act as tender to the larger vessel, and her history is scarcely less remarkable than that of the little vessel *Norfolk*, Flinders' old command, which by this time had been run away with by convicts, and "piled up" on a beach near Newcastle, New South Wales.

The *Investigator* sailed, and Flinders made Cape Leeuwin on September 7th, 1801. He ran along the south and east coasts, met the Baudin expedition in Encounter Bay, and entered Port Phillip on April 26th, 1802, and found that the *Lady Nelson* had preceded him in the February before. Arriving in Sydney in May, he sailed again a couple of months later to the northward, surveying the Great Barrier Reef, Torres Straits, the Gulf of Carpentaria, and the coast of Arnhem's Land. By this time the ship was too unseaworthy to prosecute further work, so Flinders sailed round the entire continent by way of the Leeuwin, and finally arrived in Sydney harbour again in June, 1803.

In these voyages he performed exploring work that is now a part of English history, and his charts of the Australian coasts were the foundation of all others that have since been made. He either first used the name of Australia or adapted it to the great continent, and New Holland, after the publication of his charts, began to be a name of the past.

Most of the remainder of this story can best be told in the words of Flinders and from the narratives of his officers.

1805

The long and rough voyage of the *Investigator* had shaken her poor old carcase terribly, as the following summary of an examination by the captains of the men-of-war then in Sydney Harbour and others will show:—

> "On the port side out of ninety-eight timbers, eleven were sound, and sixty-three were uncertain if strained a little; on the starboard five out of eighty-nine timbers were good, fifty-six were uncertain, and twenty-eight rotten; the planking about the bows and amidships was so soft that a stick could be poked through it."

Considering all these defects it was not worth while to keep her, so she was converted into a hulk in Sydney Harbour. But later on it was found that by cutting her down it might be possible to navigate her to England. This was done, and the old ship sailed from Sydney on May 24th, 1805, under the command of Captain Kent, who managed with the greatest difficulty to reach Liverpool on the 14th of October following. In his despatch announcing her arrival he says:—

> "A more deplorable, crazy vessel than the *Investigator* is, perhaps, not to be seen. Her maintopmast is reefed a third down; we have been long without topgallantmasts, being necessitated to take the topgallant rigging for running gear."

And Governor King, anxious to do Flinders justice, says:—"I hope no carping cur will cast any reflection on him respecting the *Investigator* . . . should it be so it will be an act of great injustice," and then he alludes to the thoroughly rotten condition of the ship. He was quick, too, to recognize the immense value of the work accomplished by Flinders, and made him every offer of help that lay within his power to continue the survey.

There were not more than half a dozen vessels in the colony, but Flinders could have any one of them he liked, but they were all too small and unfit for such a severe service. At last it was decided that he should return home as a passenger in the *Porpoise*; some of his fellow-workers on the *Investigator* accompanied him, others went to the East Indies, and one or two stayed behind. It was with a feeling of intense satisfaction that Flinders took possession of his comfortable cabin on the *Porpoise*, for he was looking forward to an agreeable rest after the hardships he had undergone. The quarter-deck was taken up by a greenhouse protecting the plants collected on the *Investigator's* voyage, and designed for the King's garden at Kew.

Early in August, accompanied by two returning transports, the *Cato* and *Bridgewater*, the *Porpoise*, under Lieutenant Fowler, sailed out of Sydney Harbour, and steered a northerly course along the coast, closely followed by the other two ships. With Flinders on board to consult, Fowler had no fear of the dangers of the Barrier Reef, and with a lusty south-east breeze, and a sky of cloudless blue, the three ships pressed steadily northward. Four days later they arrived at a spot about 730 miles north of Sydney, just abreast of what is now Port Bowen, on the Queensland coast.

It was the second dog-watch, the evening was clear, and the three ships were slipping slowly over the undulating Pacific swell. Flinders was below chatting to his friends about old times, and the officers were having a quiet smoke, when a cry of "Breakers ahead!"

from both the quarterdeck and forecastle rang out in the quiet night. The helm was put down, but the vessel had not enough way on, and scarce brought up to the wind. Flinders, for the moment thinking he was on board the old *Investigator* again, turned to the officer near him and said with a quiet smile: "At her old tricks again; she wants as much tiller rope as a young wife."

A few minutes later he rose and went on deck to look around. The cry of "Breakers ahead!" had nothing alarming in it to him, so he had not hurried; but one quick glance showed him that the ship was doomed, for the breakers were not a quarter of a cable's-length away, and the inset of the swell was rapidly hurrying the ship to destruction. Two minutes later a mountain sea lifted the *Porpoise* high, and took her among the roaring surf. In another moment she struck the coral reef with a thud that shook her timbers from keel to bulwarks; then the ship fell over on her beam ends in the savage turmoil, her deck facing inshore. So sudden was the catastrophe that no one could fire a gun for help or for warning to the other ships, which were following closely. As the ship rolled over on her beam ends, huge, thundering seas leapt upon and smothered her, and the darkness of the night was accentuated by the white foam and spume of the leaping surf. In a few moments the foremast went, the bottom was stove in, and all hope was abandoned; and then during a momentary lull in the crashing breakers they saw the *Cato* and *Bridgewater* running directly down upon the *Porpoise*. For some seconds a breathless, horror-struck silence reigned; then a shout arose as the two transports shaved by the stricken ship and were apparently saved.

But their rejoicing was premature, for a minute or two later the *Cato* struck upon an outlying spur of the reef, not a cable-length away. Like the *Porpoise*, she at once fell over on her side, but with her deck facing the sweeping rollers, and each succeeding wave spun her round and round like a top and swept her fore and aft. The *Bridgewater* escaped, and a light air enabled her to stand to the north out of danger.

Flinders at once took command on the *Porpoise*, a small gig was lowered to leeward, and with half a dozen men, two odd, short oars, and shoes and hats for balers, he set out to struggle through the breakers to a calm ring of water beyond, where they might find a sandbank to land upon, or get within hailing distance of the *Bridgewater*. Meanwhile Fowler was thinking of lightening the *Porpoise* and letting her drive further up on the reef; but fear was expressed that she might be carried over its inside edge, and founder in 17 fathoms of water. The two cutters were launched, and stood by under the lee of the ship throughout the long, weary night in case she broke up. At intervals of half an hour, blue lights flared over the dismal scene, and lit up the strained, white faces of those watching for the lights of the ship that was safe, and which, either not seeing or not heeding their distress, had disappeared from view.

During the night the wind blew high and chill, the sea increased in fury, and the ship groaned and shuddered at each fresh onslaught. Fowler, however, was hard at work constructing a raft, ready for launching at dawn, and his men, exhausted as they were, bore themselves as do most British seamen in the hour of death and danger.

Flinders meanwhile had succeeded in reaching the lagoon within the reef, and he and his men jumped out of the boat, and walked to and fro in the shallow water to keep themselves warm and out of the wind; but they sought in vain to discern the lights of the *Bridgewater*. But the *Bridgewater* had sailed on to meet another fate. She reached India safely, then left again for England, and was never afterwards heard of. It is difficult to understand how her people could have avoided seeing the others' distress; it is harder still to believe that, seeing their plight, the *Bridgewater's* company could have thus deserted the castaways. Of course, this explanation would have been demanded, but the *Bridgewater* was an "overdue" ship long before the news of the disaster arrived in England.

As the sun rose, the scene looked less hopeless, and the men found that they were near a small sandbank, on which were a quantity of seabirds' eggs. Close by were the *Porpoise* and *Cato* still holding together on the reef. Returning to the former ship, Flinders at once sent a boat to rescue the exhausted crew of the *Cato*, who flung themselves into the waves, and were picked up safely.

Then all hands from both wrecks—marvellous to say, only three men were lost during the night—set to work under his directions, and collected all the food and clothing they could possibly obtain. With the warmth of the sun their spirits returned, and the brave fellows took matters merrily enough, many of them decking themselves out in the officers' uniforms, for their own clothing could not be reached. A landing was soon effected, and a topsail yard was set up as a flagstaff, with the blue ensign upside down, though but little hope was entertained of passing vessels in such a place. In all there were 94 people under Flinders' care, and they made themselves comfortable in sailcloth tents on the barren sand spit. Enough food had been saved from the *Porpoise* to last for three months; but to Flinders' grief many of the papers, charts, and pictures dealing with his explorations were sadly damaged. Among the articles saved was a picture of Government House, Sydney, in 1802, and this and some others are now in the possession of the Royal Colonial Institute, London.

The bank upon which the castaways lived was only 150 fathoms long by 50 broad, and about 3 feet above water. Whilst looking for firewood some of Flinders' men found an old sternpost of a ship of about 400 tons, which he imagined might have belonged to one of the ships of the La Pérouse expedition.

Wearily enough the time passed, and then Flinders determined to attempt to reach Sydney in one of the ship's boats. He chose a six-oared cutter, and raised her sides with such odd timber as he could find. She was christened *The Hope*, and on the 26th August he with the commander of the *Cato*, 12 seamen, and three weeks' provisions, bade farewell to their comrades, and with a cheer, set out with bold hearts upon their voyage.

VIEW OF WRECK REEF

The Hope reached Sydney safely on the 8th September, and Flinders and his companions went straight to Government House, where King was having dinner. The Governor leapt from his chair with astonishment, almost taking them for spectres, so half starved and distressing was their appearance.

"But," says Flinders, "as soon as he was convinced of the truth of the vision, and learned the melancholy cause, a tear started from the eye of friendship and compassion, and we were received in the most affectionate manner."

Alas for poor Flinders! There were yet in store for him worse miseries, and tears of sorrow from those nearer and dearer to him were yet to flow in abundance in the many weary years of waiting yet to come.

CHAPTER IX.

THE CAPTIVITY OF FLINDERS

In Governor King, Flinders had a firm friend, and one who sympathized deeply with his misfortune, as was soon evinced. But the first thing to be done was to rescue the castaways on Wreck Reef, as Flinders had named the scene of the disaster, and the master of the ship *Rolla*, bound to China, was engaged by King to call at the reef with provisions and convey to Canton all those of the ships' companies who preferred going to that port; and the *Francis*, a schooner of 40 tons, sent in frame from England in 1792, was to accompany the *Rolla* and bring back those of the shipwrecked men who chose to return to Port Jackson.

But for Flinders himself King did more: he offered him the use of a small vessel to sail to England to convey home the charts and journals of the *Investigator* voyage. The vessel was named the *Cumberland*; she was only 29 tons, and had been built in Sydney, but Flinders was satisfied that she was capable of performing the voyage; and both he and King, being men of action, decided that she should sail, in company with the *Francis* and *Rolla*, to the scene of the wreck, where Flinders was to select officers and men to man her for the voyage to England, a temporary crew being given him for the run down to the reef. King told Flinders to choose his own route for the voyage home, to sell the little vessel at the Cape or elsewhere if he thought fit, and engage another to continue the voyage, and, in fact, gave his friend a free hand.

The Australian press of the day consisted of the *Sydney Gazette*, then in its first year of existence, and sometimes printed on odd scraps of wrapping paper by reason of the shortness of other material, and this paper, speaking of the *Cumberland*, says,

"She is a very good sea-boat, and in every way capable of carrying enough water and provisions for Captain Flinders and the officers and nine men who are appointed to navigate the first vessel built in the colony to England."

Nevertheless there were many naval men who thought the venture dangerous in the extreme, and sought to dissuade Flinders from undertaking it. But his was no timorous nature—"a small craft, 'tis true," he said laughingly, "but mine own."

With all papers necessary to prove his identity and his dearly-loved journals and charts on board, Flinders bade farewell to his trusty friend King, and on September 21st, 1803, the three vessels, the lumbering *Rolla* and the two midgets of schooners, put to sea. Before midnight, just after leaving Port Jackson, the three ships were flying before a south-easterly gale, and the *Cumberland* was reduced to a close-reefed mainsail and jib, and she was so exceedingly crank that Flinders considered it was not safe to run her even in a double-reefed topsail breeze. Then, in spite of her recent repairs, she leaked like a basket, and after an hour and a half's cessation from pumping the water was awash on the cabin floor. But nevertheless she was more weatherly than either the *Rolla* or *Francis*, for in working to windward at night-time Flinders would have to run down four miles or so in the morning to join them, although they carried all the sail they possibly could.

A fortnight later they arrived at Wreck Reef, and when Flinders sent King an account of the trip down, he gave the Governor some idea of the discomforts experienced. He wrote in a humorous vein:—

> "Of all the filthy little things I ever saw, this schooner, for bugs, lice, fleas, weevils, mosquitos, cockroaches, large and small, and mice, rises superior to them all . . . I have never stripped myself before the last two nights, but usually slept upon the lee locker with my clothes on . . . I believe that I, as well as my clothes, must undergo a good boiling in the large kettle."

In the evening of the 7th October the three vessels anchored under the lee of Wreck Island, to the great joy of its tenants, and as soon as Flinders landed on the bank they gave him three cheers and fired a salute from the carronades saved from the wreck. The *Porpoise* still held together, and the castaways had, during Flinders' absence, built a boat of 20 tons, which they had rigged as a schooner and named the *Resource*, and on that very day some of them were out sailing her on her trial trip. This little vessel Flinders sent to King as some compensation for the *Cumberland*.

As soon as possible the shipwrecked men embarked, some on the *Rolla* for China, the rest on the *Francis* and *Resource* for Sydney; then Flinders said goodbye and sailed northward for Timor, where he arrived thirty days later. Here he wrote again to King; then came another letter dated from the Mauritius, August 8th, 1804:—

> "Thus far, my dear sir, I had written to you from Coupang, in case of meeting a ship by which it might have been sent, little expecting that I should have finished it here, and in a prison.
>
> "We found the upper works of the schooner constantly leaky, and the pumps became so much worn by constant use as to be rendered unserviceable, and made it absolutely necessary to put in at this island to get the schooner caulked and the pumps refitted before attempting the passage round the Cape of Good Hope. I also considered that, in case of a new war, I had no passports from the Dutch, as well as that by putting in here I should be able to ascertain how far the French settlements in this neighbourhood might answer your purpose of supplying Port Jackson with cattle. Having no chart or instructions relating to Mauritius, I came round the south end of the island, and followed a small vessel that I wanted to speak into a little harbour there" (Baye du Cap), "and, to my surprise, found that the French were again at war with our nation. After being detained one day I got a pilot, and came round to Port N.W." (Port Louis) "on December 16th last. I waited upon the captain-general, and, after being kept two hours in the street, had an audience, but it was to be told that I was an imposter, the improbability of Captain Flinders coming in so small a vessel being thought so great as to discredit my passport and commission. Finally, Mr. Atkin, formerly master of the *Investigator*, and me were brought ashore as prisoners at 2 o'clock in the morning, all my books and papers were taken

away, and a sentinel with fix't bayonet was placed in the room where we lodged. After undergoing an examination next day, I thought circumstances were going in my favour, but in three days an order was issued to put my seamen on board the prison-ship, the vessel's stores in the arsenal, and the schooner to be laid up. As for Mr. Atkin and me, we continued in the house of our confinement, but with this difference, that the sentinal was placed without side of our room, and I was permitted to have my servant, and afterwards obtained my printed books and some unfinished charts upon which to employ myself.

GOVERNMENT HOUSE, SYDNEY, IN 1802

"I expostulated with General de Caen upon this uncommon and very harsh treatment, but could obtain no satisfaction or public information than that I had deviated from the voyage for which the passport had been granted by touching at the Isle of France, and that my uncommon voyage from Port Jackson to this place was more calculated for the particular interests of Great Britain than for those of my voyage of discovery. In fine, I was considered and treated as a spy, and given to understand that my letters gave great offence.

"I became very ill in this confinement, the scurvy breaking out in my legs and feet. A surgeon was sent to attend me, but altho' he represented the necessity of taking exercise, yet was I not permitted to take a walk outside in the air for near four months, or was any person allowed to speak to me without the general's permission. Through the intercession of the excellent Captain Bergeret, of the French navy, I was removed to the house where the English officers, prisoners of war, were confined. This house is situated a little without the town, enjoys a pure air, and is surrounded by a wall enclosing about two acres of ground. In this place Mr. Atkin and me soon recovered our health, and here we have remained to this day. Thro' my friend Bergeret, I have lately obtained the greatest part of my books and charts, and therefore am assiduously employed in repairing the ravages that were made amongst them by the *Porpoise's* shipwreck, and in making others to complete the hydrographical account of my voyage. Admiral Linois, as well as Bergeret and another naval captain, interested themselves that I might be sent to France, but it was positively refused, upon the principle that I must wait until orders were received concerning me from the French Government; and an application to be sent into the interior part of the island, where we might enjoy good exercise and some society, was no more successful.

"This account will not a little surprise you, my dear sir, who have so lately shown every attention to the *Geographe* and *Naturaliste*; but a military tyrant knows no law or principle but what appears to him for the immediate interest of his Government or the gratification of his own private caprices. Passports, reciprocal kindness, and national faith are baits to catch children and fools with, and none but such consider the propriety of the means by which the plans are to be put into execution. Men of genius, heroes (that is, modern French generals), are above those weaknesses. I can give you no further explanation of General de Caen's conduct except that he sent me word I was not considered to be a prisoner of war, and also that it was not any part of my own conduct that had occasioned my confinement.

"What I am suffering in promotion, peace of mind, fortune, fame, and everything that man holds dear, it is not my intention to detail, or have I room; but when added to shipwreck and its subsequent risks, they make no very common portion of suffering. How much I deserve all this may be left to your friendly judgement to decide. It is impossible for me to guess how long I am to be kept here, since the French despatches, as well as the letters I have been permitted to write, will probably be thrown overboard on the ship meeting with our cruisers. However, I think my foe begins to be touched with some remorse of conscience. We have accounts by Admiral Linois of the China fleet having lately passed, and in it my officers and people, who, I hope, are before this time in England. Having a private opportunity of sending a letter to India, I commit this to the care of Mr. Campbell for you; and may you, my kind friend, and yours never feel to know the unlimited power of a man before whom innocence and hardship are of no avail to save from his severity."

In Flinders' book we are told that the explorer, when ordered by petty officials to remain in Baye du Cap with the *Cumberland* until General de Caen's pleasure was known, said: "I will do nothing of the kind; I am going to Port Louis overland, and I shall take my commission, passport, and papers to General de Caen myself." The officers were a little crestfallen, but the Englishman's short, precise, active manner left nothing to be said, so he went on shore in his simple, severe, threadbare, brine-stained coat, as though Matthew Flinders, of the *Cumberland*, 29 tons, His Majesty's exploring vessel, was fully the equal of any hectoring French governor-general.

While waiting in an ante-room to see the governor, some French military officers came in, and began to talk to the Englishman, asking him, among other things, if he had ever come across "M. Flinedare, who was not unknown to fame." It took him some time to find out that it was himself. At last an interpreter took him into the governor's reception room, where, without preface, de Caen brusquely said: "Where is your passport and your commission; and why did you come without the *Investigator*?"

"She was so rotten fore and aft that she crumbled at a touch," was the reply.

"Have you an order to come to this isle? Why did you come?"

"Necessity made me," answered Flinders calmly.

"You are imposing, sir," angrily replied de Caen; "you know it is not possible that the governor of New South Wales would send you out in so small a boat. Take him away, and treat him well," he added, turning to the guard, and this was Flinders' last hour of freedom for years to come.

His quarters, shared with Atkin at first, were in a small house, part of a café, "under the dark entry, and up the narrow stairs into a bedroom, while the door was bolted, and the regular tramp, tramp, of the sentry kept on hour after hour."

It was a meagre room, containing two truckle-beds, two rush-bottomed chairs, a broken old gilt-bordered looking-glass, and evil smells. At 6 a.m. the sleeping men were wakened by the patrol of an armed grenadier in the bedroom—a needless annoyance. The meals of fresh meat, bread, fruit, and vegetables were a luxury.

Monistrol, the colonel commanding the garrison, a few days later took Flinders to the home of General de Caen, whose secretary again asked why his vessel was so small. Where were his scientific men, why did he go to Port Northwest at all, and why did he chase a vessel? (This query referred to his endeavour to overtake a pilot-boat.) He gave his reasons in full, and expected to be allowed to go back to the *Cumberland*. Shortly afterwards a message came from the governor asking him to dinner, but he refused, saying, "Unless I am a free man, I will not come to the governor's table."

On July 12th, 1804, he wrote to Sir Joseph Banks:—

> "Since my imprisonment in this island I have written to you, Sir Joseph, several letters, and by several conveyances. Some of them must no doubt have been received. General de Caen still keeps me closely confined, but he has lately given me the greater part of my books and papers, and, therefore, I shall again be able to proceed in preparing the accounts of our discoveries.
>
> "I have now been kept in prison seven months. The time passes drearily along, and I have yet to remain five

months longer before any orders are likely to be received concerning me from the French Government; and then it is uncertain of what nature they may be, since it is not known what statement the General has made of my particular case; and probably the vessels carrying the despatches will be taken, and the letters thrown overboard, in which case it cannot be guessed how long I may be kept. My dependence, therefore, is on the Admiralty demanding me to be given up, by virtue of the French passport, in which, even here it is acknowledged, there has been no infringement on my part further than in intention, which intention has been misconstrued and misunderstood by a man violent against the name of an Englishman, and ignorant of what relates to voyages of discovery.

"This arbitrary man is now doing me the greatest injury without even making a plea for it. His own subjects (for he is a most despotic monarch), Frenchmen, who are acquainted with the circumstances, condemn him for it; but the generality cannot believe that the commander of a voyage of discovery, whose labour is calculated for the good of all nations, should be kept a prisoner without something greatly wrong on his part; and, since no crime is charged against me, it is currently reported here that I have not the requisite papers to prove my identity.

"I hope, Sir Joseph, that, even from the charts which I have sent home, you will think we did as much as the lateness of the season with which we first came upon the coast, and the early rottenness of the *Investigator* could well allow; and I think our labours will not lose on a comparison with what was done by the *Geographe* and *Naturaliste*. No part of the unfortunate circumstances that have since occurred can, I believe, be attributed to my neglects or mistakes; and therefore I am not without hope that, when the Admiralty know I am suffering an unjust imprisonment, they will think me worthy to be put upon the post-captains' list. My age now exceeds the time at which we judge in the navy a man ought to have taken his station there who is to arrive at anything eminent. It would soften the dark shade with which my reflections in this confinement cannot but be overspread to know that I was promoted to the list where my rank would be progressive. It is to you only, Sir Joseph, that I can address upon this subject. I have had ample testimonies of your power and of the strength of your mind in resisting the malicious insinuations of those who are pleased to be my enemies, nor do I further doubt your willingness to give me assistance than that I fear you do not yet think me worthy of it; but I will be. If I do not prove myself worthy of your patronage, Sir Joseph, let me be thrown out of the society of all good men. I have too much ambition to rest in the unnoticed middle order of mankind. Since neither birth nor fortune have favoured me, my actions shall speak to the world. In the regular service of the navy there are too many competitors for fame. I have therefore chosen a branch which, though less rewarded by rank and fortune, is yet little less in celebrity. In this the candidates are fewer, and in this, if adverse fortune does not oppose me, I will succeed; and although I cannot rival the immortalized name of Cook, yet if persevering industry, joined to what ability I may possess, can accomplish it, then will I secure the second place, if you, Sir Joseph, as my guardian genius, will but conduct me into the place of probation.

"But this is visionary, for I am so fast in prison that I cannot get forth. The thought is bitterness. When I recollect where and what I am, and compare it with where and how I ought to be employed, it is misery; but when to this the recollection of my family and the present derangement of their affairs from my absence are added, then it is that the bonds enter deep into my soul."

While his money lasted, Flinders spent it in buying fruit and vegetables for his imprisoned crew; when cash ran out, he drew a bill on the Admiralty. The interpreter who undertook to get it cashed was nearly killed by the soldiers for carrying, as they thought, a private letter. Eventually the Danish consul cashed this bill for the Englishmen, and gave them full value for it, which, considering the state of the times, shows that he was a truly good man.

The *Cumberland* was taken to the head of the harbour and converted into a hulk, and a document was brought to Flinders to sign in which—in truly French fashion—he was asked to accuse himself of being a spy. He promptly refused the request, which was again and again made, and he always scorned to comply. While his papers were being overhauled, Flinders managed to secure some of them, and among other things the signal-book, which he destroyed.

De Caen's report to his Government shows the view he took of these proceedings. In it he says:—

> "Commander Flinders, formerly captain of the corvette *Investigator*, sent by the English Government for work of discovery in the Pacific Ocean, has altered absolutely the mission for which he had obtained from the French Government the passport signed by the Minister for Marine. In such passport he is certainly not authorized to land at the Isle of France to study the prevailing winds, the port, or the state of the colony, and by this conduct he has violated the neutrality under which he had been permitted to land. It is necessary therefore to order M. Monistrol, chief of the battalion, to board the schooner *Cumberland* in the presence of Captain Flinders, break the seals put on his room, and gather certain papers which may be required to complete proofs already in existence of the charge against him. The room is then to be resealed, and Captain Flinders to be taken back to the house where he has already been confined as prisoner. The crew of the schooner are meanwhile to be kept prisoners on the prison-ship."

Flinders wrote repeatedly by every vessel into which he could smuggle a letter, to Banks, to King, and to his superiors in England. Many of these letters never arrived, but what letters did reach home aroused the indignation of his friends; and Sir Joseph Banks in England, King in Sydney, and many others worked hard to effect the release of the prisoner.

To de Caen Flinders wrote several letters, giving him some "straight talk." Here are some extracts:—

> "If you say it is a breach of neutrality to come here for the reasons I did, how is it that when your discoverers put into Port Jackson, etc., they were received well? In war-time Baudin and Hamelin took notes, and were not interfered with ... I was chosen by Sir Joseph Banks to

complete Cook's work, and am not a spy. If I had come as a spy, what have I done? Why not wait till the eve of sailing to arrest me? I have been a prisoner since the first hour I landed."

VIEW OF SYDNEY

1804

The governor's answer was—

"It is useless to get up a discussion, as you do not appreciate the delicate motive of my silence. I say, until matters are advanced more, say nothing, as you know so little of the rules of good manners."

This rude letter maddened Flinders. He wrote another long epistle, setting forth reasons for letting him go, even to France, promising to say not a word of Mauritius and stating again the absolute simple necessity of his visit. He could extract no answer.

The heat was fearful. All the respectable people in the place were gone to the hills, and Flinders and his men nearly died of the horrible confinement. His letters were opened, and very few reached England. At home Sir Joseph Banks set to work, and did his best for the poor prisoner. On August 29th, 1804, he (Banks) wrote to Governor King a long letter, which is full of things he was disinterestedly doing for the colony, and that letter says:—

> "Poor Flinders, you know, I suppose, put into the Isle de France for water, and was detained as a prisoner and treated as a spy. Our Government have no communication with the French; but I have some with their literary men, and have written, with the permission of the Government, to solicit his release, and have sent in my letter a copy of the very handsome one M. Baudin left with you. If this should effect Flinders' liberation, which I think it will, we shall both rejoice."

In June, 1805, Banks wrote to Flinders from London, detailing what had been done:—

> "From the moment that I heard of your detention, I have used every effort in my power towards effecting your release. As the enmity between the Governments of France and England is carried to such a height that no exchange has on any pretence been effected, they could do nothing for you. I therefore obtained permission in August last to address the National Institute of France requesting their interference to obtain your release as a literary man, a mode by which I have obtained the release of five persons from the gracious condescension of the Emperor, the only five, I believe, that have been regularly discharged from their *parole*.
>
> "My letters were unfortunately detained in Holland some months, and, in fact, did not arrive at Paris till April. I received, however, an immediate and favourable answer, which proves that the literary men in Paris will do all in their power to obtain your liberty; but, unfortunately, the Emperor of the French was in Italy, where he still remains, when my letter arrived.
>
> "I confess, however, I entertain sanguine hopes of a favourable answer, when he shall return to Paris, from the marked and laudable attention His Imperial Majesty has always shown to scientific men. As far as I know, your

friends here are well. Mrs. Flinders I heard of very lately, as full of anxiety for your return. I have heard many times from her on the subject, and always done my utmost to quiet her mind and soothe her apprehensions.

"All your letters to me and to the Admiralty have, I believe, been safely received. Your last, containing the last sheet of your chart, I forwarded to the Hydrographical Office at the Admiralty, as you desired.

"We have had a succession of First Lords of the Admiralty since Lord Spencer, no one of them favourable to the pursuit of discovery, and none less than the present Lord Barham, late Sir Charles Middleton. As he, however, is eighty-four years old, either his mind or his body must soon become incapable of any exertion whatever. I have no news to tell you relative to discovery. M. Baudin's voyage has not yet been published. I do not hear that his countrymen are well satisfied with his proceedings. Captain Bligh has lately been nominated governor of New South Wales."

Meanwhile prizes taken by the French were coming into the Mauritius, and there were many English prisoners on the island. Their detention became a little less wearisome with work, music, billiards, astronomy, and pleasant companionship. It was a curious company. Prisoners who were gathered from many parts of the world and grades of society strove only to make the time pass easily, and succeeded until de Caen heard of this and ordered, in his usual haughty style, that "spy-glasses and such things" should be taken away, and if anything were concealed, then the prisoners were to be kept in close confinement, and if they showed themselves outside of the house, were to be shot. Their swords were demanded. Flinders refused to give his up to the petty officer sent to receive it. "Very well," said the inconsistent de Caen, "as he is not a prisoner, he may keep his."

In July, 1805, the captive wrote to Banks this letter:—

"My last letter to you was dated May 16th, and sent by Mr. Atkin, the master of the *Investigator*, who, having obtained his leave to depart, took his route by the way of America. He had not been gone many days when an English squadron of four ships appeared off this island,

and they are now cruising round it; and about a fortnight since two cartels arrived here with French prisoners from Calcutta and Ceylon. In return for these, all the prisoners of war in this island are to be sent back, and I only to be excepted. It seems that, notwithstanding my imprisonment has continued near nineteen months, the French governor has not received orders from his Government as to the disposal of my person and papers. They have told him he did right to detain and secure me; but their final decision is deferred to their next despatches. These are expected very soon, and then possibly I may be either liberated, or sent to France to be tried as a spy.

1805

"The French captain Bergeret, who arrived from Calcutta, professes to be much interested for me; and, since he has influence with General de Caen, it is possible that I may obtain some little indulgence of liberty after my countrymen are gone. Both justice and humanity ought to have obtained this at least for me before; but it seems to be only to private favour and party interest that any concession is made by this arbitrary general.

"Upon the supposition that the first despatches from France will occasion my removal, I expect to be in England or in France, upon a reasonable computation, about February or March, 1806, at which time I anxiously hope and pray that I may find you, my best and most powerful friend, in the possession of health and happiness, and my country enjoying the sweets that must arise from an honourable peace.

"Had I been permitted to go to India with the other prisoners, it was my intention to have applied to Sir Edward Pellew for a ship to go upon the north-west coast of New Holland, to ascertain the existence of an entrance into an inland sea, near the Rosemary Isles of Dampier, previously to my return to Europe, for during the continuance of such a war as the present, I can scarcely hope to get a ship in England to complete the *Investigator's* voyage. This project, however, is now dissipated."

And again in November of the same year he wrote:—

> "I have already informed you of a permission I received, after the departure of all the prisoners of war, to leave my place of confinement, and reside in the country on account of my health. I have now for nearly three months resided in this district, almost in the middle of the island, with a very agreeable and respectable family, from whom I receive every kindness and attention, and with the permission to extend my walks six miles round.
>
> "Since my residence in this district I have not had the least communication with General de Caen, but the liberty I now enjoy is a sufficient proof that he has ceased to consider me as a spy; and I firmly believe that, if he had not said to the French Government during the time of his unjust suspicions of me that he should detain me here until he received their orders, he would have gladly suffered me to depart long since, for he has the character of having a good heart, though too hasty and violent."

By this time all other prisoners had been exchanged, and Flinders alone, with an old, lame seaman (his servant) were the only English remaining.

It was not altogether wonderful that the captive should be forgotten. Trafalgar was fought while Flinders was a prisoner, and in Europe people could hardly be expected to remember one solitary prisoner of the French so far away.

1807

What delay was in those days may be seen from the fact that a letter arrived on July 18th, 1807, from Sir Edward Pellew, commanding the *Duncan*, Madras Roads, June 21st, stating that papers had been really sent for the captive's release. A private letter was enclosed inviting Flinders to come and stop in India with Pellew. The copy of the letter Flinders received drove the resentment deeper into his heart, for it stated that the Paris authorities approved of de Caen's action, but granted Flinders liberty in pure generosity. In July, 1804, this letter had been approved by the authorities; in March, 1806, it had been signed by the Emperor; and in July, 1807, it had arrived in Mauritius, and yet the copy that left London in December reached Mauritius first. Flinders wrote again to de Caen, and was told to "wait a bit." Was ever such an unfortunate man as Matthew Flinders?

In December, 1809, when Flinders had been prisoner in the island seven years, the English blockaded the port, and the Englishmen were kept closer than ever. Then arrived the *Harriet* to exchange prisoners, and in March of the following year Flinders was informed that he was to be one of the men exchanged. But it was actually July, 1810, before the *Harriet* got away, for the English, not knowing that they were detaining their own countrymen, kept such a close blockade that the ship could not get out to sea; and when she did get outside, notwithstanding many attempts on the part of the captain to communicate with an English ship and put Flinders on board, he could not overtake one. It turned out afterwards that the English fleet had heard of Flinders being on board the *Harriet* and gave her a wide berth, thinking that by this means the French would understand that she was at liberty to pursue her way to Europe and land Flinders without molestation from his countrymen.

Ultimately Flinders reached the Cape of Good Hope, and from thence England. When he arrived he received a warm enough welcome from his relatives and immediate friends, but the public had too many stirring events to talk about to think of him, and so publicly his services were practically forgotten. Among other indignities he suffered, he found that the charts taken from him by de Caen had been appropriated to Baudin's exploring expedition. The remainder of his life he devoted to writing his book, *An Account of a Voyage to Terra Australia*, which was published on the very day of his death (July 14th, 1814). Almost his last words were:—

"I know that in future days of exploration my spirit will rise from the dead, and follow the exploring ships."

1814

Flinders had married in 1801 Ann, daughter of Captain Chappell, and by her he had one daughter, Mrs. Annie Petril, who was in 1852 granted, by the joint Governments of New South Wales and Victoria, a pension of £200 a year, which she enjoyed until her death in 1892.

CHAPTER X.

BLIGH AND THE MUTINY OF THE "BOUNTY"

Bligh arrived in New South Wales, and relieved King as governor, in August, 1806. His two years' administration in the colony is noteworthy for nothing but the remarkable manner of its termination. Just as Sir John Franklin's name will live as an Arctic explorer and be forgotten as a Tasmanian governor, so will the name of Bligh in England always recall to mind the *Bounty* mutiny and scarcely be remembered in connection with Australian history.

1806

Any number of books, and a dozen different versions, have been written of the mutiny. There is Sir John Barrow's *Mutiny of the "Bounty,"* which, considering that the author was Secretary to the Admiralty, ought to be, and is, regarded as an authority; there is Lady Belcher's *Mutineers of the "Bounty,"* by far the most interesting, and probably, notwithstanding a strong anti-Bligh bias, an impartial account of facts. It is no wonder Lady Belcher was no admirer of Bligh. Heywood, the midshipman who was tried for his life, was her step-father, and she had very good reason to remember Bligh with no friendly feeling. There are other books, some of them as dull as they are pious and inaccurate, others containing no quality of accuracy or piety, and only dull; and there is Bligh's own narrative of the affair, remarkable for its plain account of the mutiny and the writer's boat voyage and the absence of a single word that could throw a shadow of blame upon the memory of Captain Bligh.

Byron's poem of "The Island" is, of course, founded on the *Bounty* mutiny, but the poet has used his licence to such an extent that the poem, which, by the way, some of the poet's admirers say is one of his worst, has no resemblance to the facts. In 1884 Judge McFarland, of the New South Wales District Court, wrote a book on the mutiny, and this work, for the reason that it was published in a remote part of the world, is little known; yet it is probably the best book on the subject. The Judge marshals his facts with judicial ability, and he sums up in such a manner the causes leading to the mutiny, that if Bligh were on trial before him we are afraid the jury would convict that officer without leaving the box.

A critic whose opinion is entitled to the greatest weight, having read the manuscript of this and the next chapter before it went to press, considered that, although we had written of Bligh's harshness to his men as proved, we had not specifically alluded to the proof. For this reason, and because the story of the *Bounty* mutiny, like every event that happened in the South Seas a hundred years ago, is interwoven with the early history of Australia, we propose to retell the story shortly. And since it seems that Bligh's tyrannical character is still a fact not taken for granted by everyone, we will endeavour, not to justify the mutiny, but to show that, by all the rules of evidence, Bligh's behaviour to his ship's company is proved to have been of the aggravating character alleged by his shipmates, and that the *Bounty* was not, as Bligh represented her to be, what is called by sailors "a happy ship."

1776

Another reason for retelling the story is, that, notwithstanding that the name of the *Bounty* sounds most familiar in most people's ears, yet we have some evidence that the present generation has almost forgotten nearly everything relating to it.

A few years ago one of the authors went to Norfolk Island, so remote a spot that visits are counted not so many to the year, but so many years to a visitor. It was thought that an account of the descendants of the *Bounty* mutineers would be of interest to English magazine-readers. Everyone, it was supposed, knew all about the *Bounty* mutiny, so half a dozen lines were devoted to it, the rest of the space to the present state of the old Pitcairn families. The article was hawked about to most of the London magazine offices, and was invariably rejected, on the ground that no one remembered the *Bounty* mutiny, and that an account of the event would be much more acceptable. It appears from many recently printed allusions to the mutiny that the magazine editors rightly judged their public.

Bligh's first visit to the South Seas was when, under Cook, he sailed as master of the *Resolution* in 1776-9. A native of Plymouth, of obscure parentage, he was then about twenty-three years old, and had entered the service through the "hawse-pipe."

By Cook's influence, he was in 1781 promoted lieutenant, and later, through the influence of Sir Joseph Banks, was given the command of the *Bounty*, which sailed from Spithead on December 23rd, 1787, for Tahiti.

The *Bounty* was an armed transport of 215 tons burden. Her mission was to convey breadfruit to the West Indian islands, the planters having represented to George III. that the introduction of the plant would be very beneficial as an article of food. The ship was fitted up in a manner peculiar, but adapted to the service she was upon. She was 90 feet long, her greatest beam 24 feet, and her greatest depth of hold about 10 feet. This limited space was divided in the following manner: 19 tons of iron ballast and provisions and stores for the ship's total complement (46 persons) in the hold; in the cockpit cabins for some subordinate officers; on the 'tween-decks a small room for Bligh to sleep in, another for a dining and sitting-room, and a small cabin for the master. Then from right aft to the after-hatchway a regular conservatory was rigged up. Rows and rows of shelves, with garden-pots for the plants, ran all round; regular gutters were made to carry off the drainage when the plants were watered, and water being precious, the pots drained into tubs, so that the water might be used again, while special large skylights admitted air and light. On the foreside of this cabin lived the more subordinate officers, and still further forward the crew.

The crew under Bligh consisted of a master (Fryer), a gunner, boatswain, carpenter, surgeon, 2 master's mates, 2 midshipmen, 2 quarter-masters, a quarter-master's mate, boatswain's mate, a carpenter's mate and a seaman carpenter, a sail-maker, armourer, and a ship's corporal, 23 able seamen, and a man who acted as clerk and ship's steward. Besides there were two gardeners who had been selected by Sir Joseph Banks.

The *Bounty*, on her way to Tahiti, touched at Teneriffe, Simon's Bay, and at Adventure Bay, Van Diemen's Land. On arrival at Tahiti, she spent nearly five months in Matavai Bay loading the breadfruit plants. Now, according to Bligh, up to this point all had gone well on the ship, and everyone had seemed happy and contented; according to every other person on board, whether friendly or inimical to Bligh, there was a good deal of unpleasantness and discontent during the whole passage. According to Bligh, the beauty of the Tahitian women, the delightful ease and charm of island existence in contrast to the hardships of the sailor's life, tempted certain of the men into what followed; according to all other witnesses, it is admitted that the men were so tempted, that desertions took place, and the deserters were taken and severely punished before the ship left the island. But, say certain witnesses, when the mutiny broke out the seductions of Tahiti were less the cause of the outbreak than the tyrannical and coarse conduct of Bligh.

1789

In due course the ship sailed in continuation of her voyage. Then on the night of Monday, April 28th, 1789, the master, John Fryer, had the first watch, the gunner, William Peckover, the middle watch, and Fletcher Christian, the senior master's mate, the morning watch. Just as the day was breaking, when the ship was a few miles to the southward of Tofoa, one of the Friendly Island group, Bligh was rudely awakened by the entrance to his cabin of Christian and three of the crew. He was told he would be killed if he made the least noise, and Christian, armed with a cutlass, the others with muskets and fixed bayonets, escorted him to the deck, after first tying his hands behind him. The master, the gunner, the acting surgeon, Ledward (the surgeon had died and was buried at Tahiti), the second master's mate, and Nelson, one of the botanists, were at the same time secured below. The boatswain, carpenter, and clerk were allowed to come on deck, and the boatswain, acting under threats from the mutineers, hoisted out the launch.

Bligh used every endeavour, first by threats, and then by entreaties and promises of forgiveness, to induce the crew to return to their duty, and Fryer, the master, if he had received the least support, would also have made an attempt to retake the ship.

But the mutineers threatened instant death to any who attempted resistance.

The boat being hoisted out, the names of certain of the officers and crew were called, and these were ordered to enter her. Bligh was compelled to follow, and she was then dropped astern. Christian handed Bligh a sextant and a book of nautical tables, saying, as he did so, "This book is sufficient for every purpose, and you know, sir, my sextant is a good one." Four cutlasses, a 28-gallon cask of water, 150 pounds of bread, 6 quarts of rum, 6 bottles of wine, 32 pounds of pork, twine, canvas, sails, some small empty water-casks, and most of the ship's papers were put in the boat, and she was cast adrift.

At the last moment, according to Bligh, Christian, in reply to a question as to what sort of treatment was this in return for all the commander's kindness, said, "That, Captain Bligh, that is the thing: I am in hell"; according to the evidence at the court-martial, not of mutineers, but of the master and other officers who were cast adrift from the *Bounty*, what Christian did say was in reply to entreaties to reconsider what he was doing, when his words were—"No, no. Captain Bligh has brought all this on himself: it is too late; I have been in hell for weeks past."

With Bligh in the boat were eighteen persons, and twenty-five remained on the *Bounty*. The boat was 23 feet in length, 6 feet 9 inches in breadth, and 2 feet 9 inches in depth. When loaded with all these people and her stores, she had not seven inches of freeboard.

From the morning when the boat was cast adrift till forty-two days later, when her unhappy company were safely landed at Timor, Bligh's behaviour and the behaviour of those under him is a noble example of courage, endurance, and resourcefulness.

They first attempted to land at Tofoa, one of the Friendly Islands, but were driven off by the natives, and one of the seamen was killed. Bligh, therefore, resolved to land nowhere until he came to the coast of Australia, or New Holland, as it was then called.

On the twenty-eighth day they made an island off the coast, to which they gave the name Restoration. Up to this time, they had lived on such food as they had, served out in a pair of cocoa-nut shell scales, the ration being a pistol-ball's weight per man morning, noon, and night, a teaspoonful of rum or wine, and a quarter of a pint of water. Their food was occasionally varied when they were able to catch boobies. The birds were devoured raw, and the blood drunk, each man receiving his portion with the utmost fairness.

Restoration Island is one of the many little islets that stud the sea-coast from the Barrier Reef right through Torres Straits, and Bligh's people found upon it and other similar spots welcome opportunity to stretch their cramped limbs, besides obtaining fresh water, and plenty of oysters. Then they continued their journey, making their way through Torres Straits by a channel still known as Bligh's Passage, and taking a week from the time of sighting the Australian coast to the time of leaving it.

A couple of incidents that happened at this time show how it was that Bligh kept his men so well in hand. One man was sent out to look for birds' eggs; the sailor, it was discovered, had concealed some of them. Says Bligh, "I thereupon gave him a good beating. On another occasion one of the men went so far as to tell me, with a mutinous look, that he was as good a man as myself. It was not possible for me to judge where this would end if not stopped in time; therefore, to prevent such disputes in future, I determined either to preserve my command or die in the attempt, and seizing a cutlass, I ordered him to take hold of another and defend himself. On this he called out that I was going to kill him, and made concessions. I did not allow this to interfere with the harmony of the boat's crew, and everything soon became quiet."

1790-1791

On the evening of June 3rd, the twenty-third day from leaving Tofoa, they left the coast of Australia on the north-western side, and stood away for Timor, where they arrived nine days later, and were received with the greatest kindness by the Dutch officials and merchants. Their journey of about 3620 miles had taken forty-two days. One man had lost his life by the attack of savages, and Nelson, the botanist, Elphinstone, a master's mate, two seamen, and the acting surgeon, were attacked by the Batavian fever and died. Bligh and the remainder of his men secured passages home, and arrived in England in March, 1790.

In the summer of 1791 he was promoted commander, given the command of the *Providence*, with an armed tender, the *Assistance*, and sent to carry out the breadfruit transplantation idea, which he satisfactorily accomplished. But the soil of the West Indian islands would not successfully grow the fruit, and the people of the West Indies do not like it.

Meantime the *Pandora* frigate, Captain Edwards, was sent out to search for the mutineers. At Tahiti she found no *Bounty*, but two midshipmen, Heywood and Stewart, and twelve petty officers and seamen of the ship. These people gave themselves up as soon as the *Pandora* entered Matavai Bay, and they informed Captain Edwards that the *Bounty* had sailed away with the remainder of the people, no one knew whither. Two other seamen had been left behind, but one of these had murdered his comrade and a native man and child, and was himself killed by the natives for these crimes.

Stewart and Heywood, master's mate and midshipman, who were very young—the latter was fifteen at the time of the mutiny—declared to the captain of the *Pandora* that they had been detained on the *Bounty* against their wishes; but Captain Edwards believed nothing, listened to no defence. He built a round-house on the quarter deck, and heavily ironing his prisoners locked them up in this.

Stewart while on shore had contracted a native marriage, and after he had left in the *Pandora* his young wife died broken-hearted, leaving an infant daughter, who was afterwards educated by the missionaries, and lived until quite recent times.

In "Pandora's Box," as Captain Edwards' round-house came to be called, the fourteen prisoners suffered cruel torture, and nothing can justify the manner in which they were treated. The frigate sailed accompanied by a cutter called the *Resolution*, which had been built by, and was taken from, the *Bounty's* people at Tahiti on May 19th, 1791, and spent till the middle of August in a fruitless search among the islands for the remainder of the mutineers. The *Pandora* then stood away for Timor, having lost sight of the *Resolution*, which Edwards did not see again until he reached Timor.

On August 28th the ship struck a reef, now marked on the chart as Pandora's Reef, and became a total wreck. All this time the prisoners had been kept in irons in the round-house. The ship lasted until the following morning, when the survivors—for thirty-five of the *Pandora's* crew and four of the prisoners (among them the unfortunate Stewart) were drowned—got into the boats and began another remarkable boat voyage to Timor. While the vessel was going down, instead of the prisoners being released, by the express order of Captain Edwards eleven of them were actually kept ironed, and if it had not been for the humanity of boatswain's mate James Moulter, who burst open the prison, they would have all been drowned like rats in a cage. This is not the one-sided version of the prisoners only, but is so confirmed by the officers of the *Pandora* that Sir John Barrow in his book says that the "statement of the brutal and unfeeling behaviour of Edwards is but too true."

There were ninety-nine survivors, divided between four boats, and they had 1000 miles to voyage. They landed at Coupang on September 19th, after undergoing the greatest suffering, aggravated in the case of the prisoners by the most wanton cruelty on the part of Edwards. From here they were sent to England for trial, arriving at Spithead on June 19th, 1792, four years and four months after they had left in the *Bounty*, of which time these poor prisoners had spent fifteen months in irons. In the following September the accused were tried by court-martial at Portsmouth Harbour. Bligh was away on his second breadfruit voyage, but he had left behind him as much evidence as he could collect that would be likely to secure conviction, and one of the officers so backed up his statements that young Heywood, a boy of fifteen, be it remembered, came near to being hanged. Bligh's suppression of facts which would have proved that the youngsters Stewart and Heywood were mere spectators at the worst of the mutiny, Sir John Barrow suggests, has "the appearance of a deliberate act of malice."

1807

The result of the trial was the just acquittal of four of the petty officers and seamen, the conviction of Heywood, of Morrison, boatswain's mate (a man of education, who had kept a diary of the whole business), and of four seamen. Three of these last, one of them seventeen years of age at the time of the mutiny, were hanged in Portsmouth Harbour. Heywood, Morrison, and a seaman named Muspratt were pardoned. It was plain that the authorities recognized the innocence of these men, for Heywood made a fresh start in the service, and served with distinction, dying a post-captain in 1831, and Morrison was drowned in the *Blenheim*, of which ship he was gunner when she foundered off the island of Rodriguez in 1807.

What had become of the *Bounty*? In March, 1809, there reached the Admiralty an extract from the log of an American whaler, commanded by Matthew Folger. This extract showed the Pitcairn Island, hitherto scarcely known and supposed to be uninhabited, had been visited by the whaler, which found thereon a white man and several half-caste families. The man was the sole survivor of the *Bounty* mutineers, and the half-caste families were the descendants of the others by their Tahitian wives. In proof of his statements, Folger brought away with him the chronometer and azimuth compass of the *Bounty*. War was then going on, and England paid little attention to the news, until in September, 1814, two frigates, the *Briton* and the *Tagus*, visited Pitcairn, when the end of the *Bounty* story was told to the commander by the sole survivor.

When the *Bounty* left Tahiti, Christian took with him Young, a midshipman; Mills, gunner's mate; Brown, one of the two botanists; and Martin, McCoy, Williams, Quintall, and Smith, seamen. These men were accompanied by five male islanders from Tahiti and Tubuai (in which last place they had attempted to form a settlement and failed), three Tahitian women, wives of the Tahitians, and ten other Tahitian women and a child.

The *Bounty* was beached and burnt, and from her remains and the island timber the mutineers built themselves homes. Soon dissensions arose, murder followed, and within a few years after landing every Englishman save Smith was dead, nearly all of them dying violent deaths. Smith changed his name to John Adams, took a Bible from the *Bounty's* library as his guide, and set to work to govern and to train his colony of half-caste children.

1829

From 1815 Pitcairn became a pet colony of the English people, and every ship that visited it brought back stories of the piety and beautiful character of its population. Smith or Adams died in 1829. He had long before been pardoned by the English Government, and the good work he began was carried on by Mr. Nobbs, one of several persons who from time to time, attracted by the story of life at Pitcairn, had managed to make their way to the island.

In 1856 the greater portion of the Pitcairn families were removed to Norfolk Island, which the English Government had abandoned as a penal settlement, giving up to them all the prison buildings as a new home.

For years after, Norfolk Island, like Pitcairn, was known as the home of the descendants of the *Bounty* mutineers, and was talked of all over the world in the same strain as that other ideal community at Pitcairn, but civilization has now worked its evil ways. No longer is Norfolk Island governed in patriarchal fashion. It has been handed over by the Imperial Government for administration by the colony of New South Wales, and in a few years longer all that will remain of its *Bounty* story will be the names of Christian, Young, McCoy, Quintall, and the rest of them—still names which indicate the "best families" of the island.

To this day it is a mystery exactly how and when Christian met his death. The sole survivor of the mutineers, Smith (*alias* Adams), when questioned, went into details regarding the desperate quarrels of his comrades, and how they came by violent deaths; but whether his memory, owing to old age, had failed him, or he had something to conceal, it is impossible now to say. However, he gave versions of Christian's death which differed materially. The generally accepted one is that he was shot by one of the Tahitians while working in the garden, but the exact place of his burial has never been revealed.

In this connection there is a curious story. An English paper called *The True Briton* of September 13th, 1796, contained the following paragraph:—

> "CHRISTIAN, CHIEF MUTINEER ON BOARD HIS MAJESTY'S SHIP 'BOUNTY.'
>
> 1796
>
> "This extraordinary nautical character has at length transmitted to England an account of his conduct in his mutiny on board the *Bounty* and a detail also of his subsequent proceedings after he obtained command of the ship, in which, after visiting Juan Fernandez and various islands in South America, he was shipwrecked in rescuing Don Henriques, major-general of the kingdom of Chili,

from a similar disaster, an event which, after many perilous circumstances, led to his present lucrative establishment under the Spanish Government in South America, for which he was about to sail when the last accounts were received from him.

"In his voyage, etc., which he has lately published at Cadiz, we are candidly told by this enterprising mutineer that the revolt which he headed on board His Majesty's ship *Bounty* was not ascribable to dislike of their commander, Captain Bligh, but to the unconquerable passion which he and the major part of the ship's crew entertained for the enjoyments which Otaheite still held out to their voluptuous imaginations. 'It is but justice,' says he, 'that I should acquit Captain Bligh, in the most unequivocal manner, of having contributed in the smallest degree to the promotion of our conspiracy by any harsh or ungentlemanlike conduct on his part; so far from it, that few officers in the service, I am persuaded, can in this respect be found superior to him, or produce stronger claims upon the gratitude and attachment of the men whom they are appointed to command. Our mutiny is wholly to be ascribed to the strong predilection we had contracted for living at Otaheite, where, exclusive of the happy disposition of the inhabitants, the mildness of the climate, and the fertility of the soil, we had formed certain connexions which banished the remembrance of old England entirely from our breasts.'"

After describing the seizure and securing of Captain Bligh's person in his cabin, Christian is made to thus conclude his account of the revolt:—

"During the whole of this transaction Captain Bligh exerted himself to the utmost to reduce the people to a sense of their duty by haranguing and expostulating with them, which caused me to assume a degree of ferocity quite repugnant to my feelings, as I dreaded the effect which his remonstrances might produce. Hence I several times threatened him with instant death unless he desisted; but my menaces were all in vain. He continued to harangue us with so much manly eloquence, that I was fain to call in the dram-bottle to my aid, which I directed to be served round to my associates. Thus heartened and encouraged, we went through the business, though, for my own part, I must acknowledge that I suffered more than words can express from the conflict of contending passions; but I had gone too far to recede; so, putting the best face on the business, I ordered the boat to be cut adrift, wore ship, and shaped our course back for Otaheite."

In each of the books by Sir John Barrow and Lady Belcher there is the following paragraph, almost word for word:—

1809

"About 1809 a report prevailed in Cumberland, in the neighbourhood of his native place, and was current for several years, that Fletcher Christian had returned home, made frequent visits to a relative there, and that he was living in concealment in some part of England—an assumption improbable, though not impossible. In the same year, however, a singular incident occurred. Captain Heywood, who was fitting out at Plymouth, happened one day to be passing down Fore Street, when a man of unusual stature, very much muffled, and with his hat drawn close over his eyes, emerged suddenly from a small side street, and walked quickly past him. The height, athletic figure, and gait so impressed Heywood as being those of Christian, that, quickening his pace till he came up with the stranger, he said in a tone of voice only loud enough to be heard by him, 'Fletcher Christian!' The man turned quickly round, and faced his interrogator, but little of his countenance was visible; and darting up one of the small streets, he vanished from the other's sight. Captain Heywood hesitated for a moment, but decided on giving up the pursuit, and on not instituting any inquiries. Recognition would have been painful as well as dangerous to Christian if this were he; and it seemed scarcely within the bounds of probability that he should be in England. Remarkable as was the occurrence, Captain Heywood attached no importance to it, simply considering it a singular coincidence."

It is of course extremely improbable that Christian managed to leave the island before the arrival of the *Topaz* (Folger's ship), and if Heywood's impression that he had seen Christian had occurred to him anywhere near the date of the *True Briton* paragraph, one might easily account for it on the ground that the *True Briton* was a sensation-loving modern daily, born before its time, and Heywood had read the paragraph. But between 1796 and 1809 was a long interval; no news had come to England of the mutineers to revive memory of the event, and the curious ignorance of the Pitcairners of the place of Christian's burial are all circumstances which leave the manner of the mutineer officer's ending by no means settled.

The Rev. Mr. Nobbs, to whom the early Pitcairners are indebted for so much, carried on the work of John Adams so well and so piously that he was sent home to England, ordained a clergyman of the Established Church, returned to Pitcairn, and then accompanied the emigrants to Norfolk Island, where he died about ten years ago.

Mr. Nobbs had a very curious history, which we reprint from the Rev. T.B. Murray's book on Pitcairn:—

> "In 1811 he was entered on the books of H.M.S. *Roebuck*; and, through means of Rear-Admiral Murray, he was, in 1813, placed on board the *Indefatigable*, naval storeship, under Captain Bowles. In this vessel the young sailor visited New South Wales and Van Dieman's Land, whence he proceeded to Cape Horn and Cape of Good Hope, and thence, after a short stay at St. Helena, he returned to England. He then left the British Navy, but after remaining a short time at home he received a letter from his old commander, offering to procure him a berth on board a ship of 18 guns, designed for the assistance of the patriots in South America. He accepted this offer, and left England early in 1816 for Valparaiso, but the Royalists having regained possession of that place, he could not enter it until 1817. He afterwards held a commission in the Chilian service, under Lord Cochrane, and was made a lieutenant in it in consequence of his gallantry in the cutting out of the Spanish frigate *Esmeralda*, of 40 guns, from under the batteries of Callao, and during a severe conflict with a Spanish gun brig near Arauco, a fortress in Chili. In

the latter encounter Mr. Nobbs was in command of a craft which sustained a loss in killed and wounded of 48 men out of 64, and was taken prisoner with the survivors by the troops of the adventurous robber General Benevideis. The 16 captives were all shot with the exception of Lieutenant Nobbs and three English seamen; these four saw their fellow prisoners led out from time to time, and heard the reports of the muskets that disposed of them. Ever afterwards he retained a vivid memory of that dreadful fusillade. Having remained for three weeks under sentence of death, he and his countrymen were unexpectedly exchanged for four officers attached to Benevideis' army. Mr. Nobbs then left the Chilian service, and in 1822 went to Naples. In his passage from that city to Messina in a Neapolitan ship, she foundered off the Lipari Islands; and, with the loss of everything, he reached Messina in one of the ship's boats. In May, 1823, he returned to London in the *Crescent*; and in the same year he sailed to Sierra Leone as chief mate of the *Gambia*, but of 19 persons who went out in that vessel none but the captain, Mr. Nobbs, and two men of colour lived to return. In June, 1824, he again went to Sierra Leone, now as commander of the same craft, and was six weeks on shore ill of fever, but it pleased God to restore him to health in time to return with her; and he resigned command on his reaching England. Meanwhile the captain of a vessel in which he had once sailed had expatiated so frequently on the happiness of the people at Pitcairn, where he had been, that Mr. Nobbs resolved to go thither if his life should be spared; and, with this object in view, he set out on the 12th of November, 1825, in the *Circassian*, bound for Calcutta, but he was detained there until August, 1827; then, after a narrow escape from shipwreck in the Strait of Sunda, he crossed the Pacific in a New York ship called the *Oceani*, went to Valparaiso, and thence to Callao, where he met a Mr. Bunker, expended £150 in refitting a launch, and made the voyage to Pitcairn."

Bligh, in his version of the *Bounty* mutiny, says that there was absolutely no cause of discontent on board the ship until the mutineers became demoralized by their long stay at Tahiti, and that he was on the best of terms with everyone on board. In proof of this, says Bligh, Christian, when the boat was drifting astern, was asked by Bligh if this treatment was a proper return for his commander's kindness, to which the mutineer answered, "That, Captain Bligh, that is the thing. I am in hell; I am in hell." Bligh on being asked by the friends of young Heywood if he thought it possible that this boy of fifteen, who had been detained against his will, could have a guilty knowledge of the mutiny, replied in writing that the lad's "baseness was beyond all description. It would give me great pleasure to hear that his friends can bear the loss of him without much concern."

Bligh's story is contradicted by all of the mutineers—that, of course, goes without saying—but here is the point: the evidence of the mutineers is practically confirmed in every particular, and Bligh's version is contradicted by the people who were with him in the boat, and these people, Bligh himself says, were loyal. One man only, Hallett, had anything to say in confirmation of Bligh's allegations regarding Heywood, and Hallett afterwards recanted and expressed his sorrow at what he had alleged against Heywood— his statements, he admitted, were made when he was not fully responsible for what he said.

Labillardiere, in his *Voyage in Search of La Pérouse*, says that one of the officers of the *Pandora* assured some of the people of the La Pérouse expedition, whom they had met at the Cape, that Bligh's ill-treatment of the *Bounty's* people was the cause of the mutiny. Fryer, the master of the *Bounty*, who, it was shown during the court-martial, had more than anyone else supported Bligh, confirmed the statement that what Christian did say when the boat was cut adrift was, in answer to the boatswain, "No. It is too late, Mr. Cole; I have been in hell this fortnight, and will bear it no longer. You know that during the whole voyage I have been treated like a dog." Further than this, the evidence given by the mutineers, and supported in all essentials by the people cut adrift in the boat, was to the effect that there had been repeated floggings; that Bligh had continually used violent and abusive language to officers and men; that he was a petty tyrant and was guilty of all sorts of mean forms of aggravation. Here is one instance: he accused officers and men, from the senior officer under him downwards, of being thieves, alleging publicly on the quarter-deck that they stole his coconuts.

1830

Against these allegations we have nothing but Bligh's narrative and the assertions, perfectly true, that he was a brave officer, who afterwards conducted a remarkable boat voyage and served with distinction under Nelson,[G] and that such a man could not be guilty of tyranny. We are here discussing the mutiny of the *Bounty*, and not the revolt in New South Wales, else against this we might remark that he was the victim of two mutinies against his rule. Bligh was not the only coarse, petty tyrant who could fight a ship well; Edwards made a boat voyage scarcely less remarkable than Bligh's, and Edwards unquestionably was a vindictive brute. However, Sir John Barrow, who, from his position as Secretary of the Admiralty, was hardly likely to make rash assertions, in his book, published about 1830, says very plainly that Bligh, upon the evidence at the court-martial, was responsible for what happened. The mutiny being admitted, the members of the court-martial had no alternative but to convict those who were not with Bligh in the boat, but those who were not proved to have taken actual part in it, who were not seen with arms in their possession, were pardoned and ultimately promoted.

There are a dozen other equally important and quite as strong facts as these to justify the view of Bligh's character taken by us; but, unless something better than Bligh's narrative and his subsequent service is quoted in reply to this side of the case, we think that a jury of Bligh's countrymen would find that if the mutineers were seduced by thoughts of Tahiti to take the ship from him three weeks after they had left the island, and were 1500 miles from it, none the less were they driven into that act by their commander's treatment of them. But, nevertheless, the memory of Bligh's heroic courage and forethought in his wonderful boat voyage from the Friendly Islands to Timor—a distance of 3618 miles—is for ever emblazoned upon the naval annals of our country, and the wrong he did in connection with the tragedy of the *Bounty* cannot dim his lustre as a seaman and a navigator.

G   After the battle of Copenhagen, Bligh, who commanded the *Glatton*, was thanked by Nelson in these words: 'Bligh, I sent for you to thank you; you have supported me nobly.'

CHAPTER XI.

BLIGH AS GOVERNOR

Bligh, at the time of his appointment to New South Wales, was in command of the *Warrior*, and in the interval between his second breadfruit voyage and the date of his governor's commission had been behaving in a manner worthy of one of Nelson's captains. In 1794 he commanded the *Alexander* (74), which, with the *Canada*, was attacked off the Scilly Isles in November by a French squadron of five seventy-fours. The *Alexander* was cut off from her consort by three Frenchmen, when Bligh sustained their attack for three hours, and was then compelled to strike his flag, having lost only 36 men killed and wounded, while the enemy's loss was 450.

Other splendid service of Bligh is related in the following letter, which was printed in the *Daily Graphic* under date London, October 28th, 1897. The letter was signed "Mary Nutting (*née* Bligh), widow of the late rector of Chastleton, Oxon., Beausale House, Warwick," and as it is a spirited defence of a naval officer whose personal character has been impugned by these present writers as well as many others, we reprint the letter in full:—

> "Sir,—There are special circumstances relating to the event of the battle of Camperdown, the centenary of which was recently commemorated, which have never been made public. One is the duel fought between the *Director* and the *Vryheid*, in which the Dutch ship was dismasted and destroyed—a naval duel at which no other ship on either side was present, or within reach or sight. On the previous day (October 11th, 1797) the English and Dutch fleets had met, fought, and the Dutch ships were dispersed, or, as you

stated, 'their line was broken.' The Dutch admiral and his ship, however, escaped, and, no doubt, would have again been seen at sea had it not been that on October 12th, 1797, the *Director* came up with the *Vryheid*, and having, after a severe struggle, first silenced and then boarded her, the Dutch admiral went on board the English ship, and gave up his sword to the captain. The captain was Captain (afterwards Admiral) W. Bligh. Strange to say, in the despatches sent home by Admiral Duncan Captain Bligh was not mentioned. I have three large water-colour pictures taken from sketches done by an artist on board the *Director* at the time of the battle, showing the *Director* coming up and attacking the *Vryheid*, the engagement at its height, and, finally, the *Vryheid* dismasted and a wreck. Bligh was a man whose service was great, and, although in due course he became an admiral, he received no special reward from his country. In his earlier years, at the age of nineteen, he was selected by Sir Joseph Banks, his friend through life, to serve with Captain Cook as master on board the *Resolution*, in the year 1774, and sailed for four years on three voyages with him. After Captain Cook's death the navigation of the ship devolved on Bligh, who brought her home. After this, for four years, as commander, he traversed unknown seas. He fought under Admiral Parker at the Doggerbank, and under Lord Howe at Gibraltar. After the battle of Copenhagen, where Bligh commanded the *Glatton*, he was sent for by Lord Nelson to receive his thanks publicly on his quarter-deck, and the words of the great hero were— 'Bligh, I thank you; you have supported me nobly.' In the time of the mutiny at the Nore, he rendered great services by his courage and energetic efforts, recalling many of the rebellious sailors to their duty and allegiance.

"After the mutiny of the *Bounty*, Bligh, with wonderful skill and courage, brought the 18 men of his crew, who had been forced with him into the *Bounty's* launch, 23 feet long by 6 feet 9 inches wide—a distance of 6318 miles[H]— safely to Timoa. No words can say too much of the care he took of them and the devotion shown in the effort to

---

H   Mrs. Nutting has here made a mistake in the distance traversed. Timoa is, of course, meant for Timor. (See page 246.)

save them. On his return to England, he was at once made post-captain as a sign of favour, and he was given two ships, the *Providence* and another, to be fitted out at his discretion, in which to accomplish the objects for which the *Bounty* was sent. This he did with perfect success. (In his absence the trial of the mutineers of the *Bounty* took place.) As to his governorship of New South Wales, let anyone read the fourth chapter of Dr. Lang's history of the colony—Lang was no partisan or connection of Bligh—which shows beyond dispute that Bligh acted, as he always did, with the most scrupulous regard to his duty and instructions, and received from time to time the written approval of the King, through Lord Castlereagh, then Secretary of State.

"It has been the pleasure of this generation to malign and misrepresent this good man and brave, not once, but continually. It originated in false statements made in the defence of two of the mutineers, Christian and Heywood, representing Bligh's severity and cruelty as being the cause of the mutiny. Yet it can be proved from the minutes of the court-martial that Heywood on his trial defended himself by swearing that he was kept on board the *Bounty* by force, and that it was 'impossible he could ever willingly have done anything to injure Captain Bligh, who had always been a father to him.' As to Christian, it can be shown that this was the third voyage he had sailed with Captain Bligh. Would a man go three times with a commander such as Bligh has been described by his enemies?

"I have no object in writing this account but love for the memory of a man who was my mother's father, and so beloved of her and his other daughters (for he had no son), that the same love and feeling were instilled into the minds of her children. It was quite recently asserted in a newspaper that 'Bligh was dismissed his ship for ill-conduct after the mutiny of the *Bounty*,' and these attacks and false statements are frequent. I know that I am asking what you may deem unusual and inconvenient, and yet I have faith in your love of justice, and desire to clear the memory of one who served his king and country as Bligh did."

Some years ago, an accomplished young lady, well known and much respected in Norfolk Island, and one of the (two or three generations removed) descendants by one side of her family from the mutineers, visited England. An anecdote of this visit was told by the lady herself to one of these authors. This lady's husband, proud of his wife, took her to England and to his home in a certain English county, where, in her honour, her husband's relatives had invited many friends, among them a dear old lady who they knew was a descendant of Bligh. "What an interesting meeting this will be!" thought they, not taking into account all the circumstances. The old lady and the young lady were duly introduced. "Dear me!" said the young lady, "and so you are the—" (mentioning the relationship) "of the tyrant Bligh!" "How dare you, the—" (again emphasising the relationship) "descendant of a base mutineer, thus speak of a distinguished officer," indignantly exclaimed the old lady. Which little anecdote shows how very emphatically there are two sides to this story.

Bligh owed his appointment as governor to Sir Joseph Banks, and a letter from Banks, dated April 19th, 1805, says that he was empowered by Lord Camden to offer the government of the colony to Bligh at a salary of £2000 a year. Bligh's "Instructions" from the Crown contained a clause which has an important bearing on his administration. It was as follows:—

> "And whereas it has been represented to us that great evils have arisen from the unrestrained importation of spirits into our said settlement from vessels touching there, whereby both the settlers and convicts have been induced to barter and exchange their live stock and other necessary articles for the said spirits, to their particular loss and detriment, as well as to that of our said settlement at large, we do, therefore, strictly enjoin you, on pain of our utmost displeasure, to order and direct that no spirits shall be landed from any vessel coming to our said settlement without your consent or that of our governor-in-chief for the time being previously obtained for that purpose, which orders and directions you are to signify to all captains or masters of ships immediately on their arrival at our said settlement, and you are, at the same time, to take the most effective measures that the said orders and directions shall be strictly obey'd and complied with."

1807

Why Bligh should have been selected to govern the colony at this particular period it is difficult to understand, unless it was that, as appears from official correspondence, Sir Joseph Banks pretty well controlled the making of Australian history at this time— nearly always, if not invariably, to the advantage of Australia.

The condition of affairs ought to have been well understood at home. Hunter and King had both harped upon it in their despatches, and lamented their inability to remedy the abuses that had grown up. They had made it no less plain that the New South Wales Regiment, so far from being a force with which to back authority, was one of the most dangerous elements in the rum-trading community of the settlement.

Letters from the Home Office indicate that this was in a measure understood, but the tenor of the despatches also shows that it was thought the evils arose less from viciousness of the governed than from want of backbone in the governors.

Bligh's character for courage and resolution may have led to his selection as a proper person to lick things into shape. It never seems to have occurred to his superiors that a man whose ship was taken from him by a dozen mutinous British seamen, if he were more forceful, resolute, tyrannical, what you will, than diplomatic in his methods, might lose a colony in which the colonists were not British sailors, but criminals and mutinous soldiers.

When Bligh landed, the principal agricultural settlements were on the banks of the rivers Hawkesbury and Nepean, and the settlers were just suffering from one of the most disastrous floods that have occurred in a country where floods are more severe than in most others. There was very little money in the colony, and the settlers carried on a legitimate system of barter by which they exchanged with each other their grain and herds. But the floods, of course, threw this system somewhat out of gear, and he who after the floods had escaped without much damage to his property had a pretty good pull upon his neighbour whose worldly belongings had been carried away by the swollen waters.

Bligh, there is no doubt, did the right thing at this time. He slaughtered a number of the Government cattle, dividing them among the more distressed colonists; and, to encourage them to go cheerfully to work to cultivate their land again and to become independent of their fellow-settlers, he promised to buy for the King's stores all the wheat they could dispose of after the next harvest, and to pay for it at a reasonable price.

1834

Dr. Lang, in his *History of New South Wales*, published about 1834, relates how an old settler said to him, "Them were the days, sir, for the poor settler; he had only to tell the governor what he wanted, and he was sure to get it from the stores, whatever it was, from a needle to an anchor, from a penn'orth o' pack-thread to a ship's cable."

This arrangement was not conducive to the interests of the rum traders, who had been in the habit of purchasing grain and compelling the growers to accept spirits in payment for it. It operated still further against them when Bligh made a tour of the colony, took a note of each settler's requirements and of what the settler was likely to be able to produce from his land; then, according to what the governor thought the farmer was likely to be able to supply, Bligh gave an order for what was most needed by the man from the King's stores.

Of course this was taking a heavy responsibility upon himself. Even colonial governments nowadays, elected by "one-man-one-vote," scarcely go so far, but the state of the settlement must be remembered. There were no shops then, and the general public of the colony, with very few exceptions, was made up of Government officials and prisoners of the Crown. But the step was a serious interference with trade—that is, the rum trade; in consequence those in "the ring" were exasperated, and its members only wanted Bligh to give them an opportunity to retaliate upon and ruin him.

1807

MacArthur, now a landed proprietor and merchant, soon after Bligh landed, paid him a visit, and reminded the new governor of an instruction sent to King that he (MacArthur) was to be given every encouragement in his endeavour to develop the pastoral resources of the colony. "Would Governor Bligh visit his estate on the Cowpasture river" (now Camden), "and see what had been done in this direction?" to which Governor Bligh, according to the report of Major Johnston's trial, replied, and with oaths: "What have I to do with your sheep and cattle? You have such flocks and herds as no man ever had before, and 10,000 acres of the best land in the country; but you shall not keep it." Here then was a declaration of war—MacArthur, too much of a trader to be a soldier, and politician enough to have enlisted on his side the English Government—which had announced its will that he should be encouraged as a valuable pioneer colonist—*versus* Bligh, so much of a warrior as to have fought beside Nelson with honour and so impolitic as to have lost his ship to a body of mutineers, some of them officers, of whose discontent, according to his own showing, he was unaware until the moment of the outbreak.

GOVERNOR BLIGH

The fight began in this fashion. MacArthur had taken a promissory note from a man named Thompson. When the note became due, a fixed quantity of wheat was to be paid for its redemption; but, subsequent to the drawing of the note, came the great flood before mentioned; wheat went to ten times its former value, and MacArthur demanded payment on the higher scale. Thompson refused payment at the current rate, alleging that he was only bound to pay for grain at the rate he received it, although his crops had not suffered by the floods. The matter came before Bligh to decide, and he gave judgment against MacArthur, who forthwith ceased to visit Government House. Then MacArthur was taken ill, Bligh called upon him, and a peaceful aspect of affairs came over the land, which lasted until early in 1807.

Bligh, in accordance with his special instructions, had issued an order by which the distillation of spirits was prohibited, and the seizure of any apparatus employed in such process enjoined. Just about this time Captain Abbott, of the New South Wales Corps, had sent orders to his London agent to send him a still. MacArthur happened to employ the same agent, who thought it a good idea to also send his other patron a still.

1808

In due time the two stills arrived, and were shown in the manifest of the ship that brought them. Bligh instructed the naval officer of the port to lodge them in the King's store, and send them back to England by the first returning ship. The still boilers were, however, packed full of medicine, and the naval officer, thinking no harm would come of it, allowed the boilers to go to MacArthur's house, lodging only the worms in the store. This happened in March. In the following October a ship was sailing for England, and the proper official set about putting the distilling apparatus on board of her, when he discovered that the coppers were still in the possession of MacArthur, who was asked to give them up. MacArthur replied that, with regard to one boiler, that was Captain Abbott's, who could do as he liked about it; but, with regard to the other, he (MacArthur) intended to send the apparatus to India or China, where it could be disposed of. However, if the governor thought proper, the governor could keep the worm and head of the still, and the copper he (MacArthur) intended to apply to domestic purposes. The governor thereupon, after the exchange of numerous letters between MacArthur and himself, caused the stills complete to be seized; and then MacArthur brought an action for an alleged illegal seizure of his property.

MacArthur was right enough on one detail of this dispute. Bligh had demanded that he should accept from an official a receipt for "two stills with worms and heads complete." As MacArthur had never had in his possession anything but two copper boilers, he naturally refused to commit himself in this fashion, and would only accept a receipt for the coppers. The naval officer accordingly took the coppers, and MacArthur took no receipt for them.

Then happened a more serious affair. MacArthur partly owned a schooner which was employed trading to Tahiti; in this vessel a convict had stowed away, and the master of the vessel had left him at the island. The missionaries wrote to Bligh complaining of this, and proceedings were begun against MacArthur by the Government to recover the penalty incurred under the settlement regulations for carrying away a prisoner of the Crown, and a bond of £900, which had been given by the owners of the vessel, was declared forfeit.

MacArthur appealed from the court to Bligh, and Bligh upheld the court's decision. MacArthur and his partners still refused to pay, and the court officials seized the vessel. MacArthur promptly announced that her owners had abandoned her, and the crew, having no masters, walked ashore. For sailors to remain ashore in a penal settlement was another breach of regulations, chargeable against the owners of the ship from which the sailors landed, provided the sailors had left the ship with the consent of the owners; and the sailors declared that the owners had ordered them to leave the schooner.

1808

MacArthur was summoned to attend the Judge-Advocate's office to "show cause." He refused to come, on the ground that the vessel was not his property, but now belonged to the Government. One Francis Oakes, an ex-Tahitian missionary, who, having disagreed with his colleagues in the islands, had turned constable, was then given a warrant to bring MacArthur from his house at Parramatta to Sydney. Oakes came back and reported that MacArthur refused to submit, and had threatened that if he (Oakes) came a second time he had better come well armed; and much more to the same purpose. Accordingly certain well-armed civil officials went back and executed the warrant, and MacArthur was brought before a bench of magistrates, over whom Atkins, the Judge-Advocate, presided, and was committed for trial.

Atkins did not know anything of law, but he had as legal adviser an attorney who had been transported, and whose character, Bligh himself said, was that of an untrustworthy, ignorant drunkard.

The court opened on January 25th, 1808. It was formed from six officers of the New South Wales Corps, presided over by the Judge-Advocate, and the court-house was crowded with soldiers of the regiment, wearing their side arms. The indictment charged MacArthur with the contravention of the governor's express orders in detaining two stills; with the offence of inducing the crew of his vessel to leave her and come on shore, in direct violation of the regulations; and with seditious words and an intent to raise dissatisfaction and discontent in the colony by his speeches to the Crown officials and by a speech he had made in the court of inquiry over the seizure of the stills. The speech complained of was to the following effect:—

> "It would therefore appear that a British subject in a British settlement, in which the British laws are established by the royal patent, has had his property wrested from him by a non-accredited individual, without any authority being produced or any other reason being assigned than that it was the governor's order; it is therefore for you, gentlemen, to determine whether this be the tenure by which Englishmen hold their property in New South Wales."

MacArthur objected in a letter to Bligh, written before the trial, to the Judge-Advocate presiding, on the ground that this official was really a prosecutor, and had animus against him. Bligh overruled the objection, on the ground that the Criminal Court of the colony, by the terms of the King's patent, could not be constituted without the Judge-Advocate. MacArthur renewed his objection when the court met; Captain Kemp, one of the officers sitting as a member of the court, supported MacArthur's view; and the Judge-Advocate was compelled to leave his seat as president.

1808

MacArthur then made a speech, in which he denounced the Judge-Advocate in very strong language, and that official called out from the back of the court that he would commit MacArthur for his conduct. Then Captain Kemp told the Judge-Advocate to be silent, and threatened to send him to gaol, whereupon Atkins ordered that the court should adjourn, but Kemp ordered it to continue sitting. The Judge-Advocate then left the court, and MacArthur called out: "Am I to be cast forth to the mercy of these ruffians?"—meaning the civil police—and added that he had received private information from his friends that he was to be attacked and ill-treated by the civilians; whereupon the military officers undertook his protection and told the soldiers in the court to escort him to the guard-room.

Then the Provost-Marshal said this was an attempt to rescue his prisoner, went at once and swore an affidavit to this effect before Judge-Advocate Atkins and three other justices of the peace, and procured their warrant for the arrest of MacArthur. This was shown to the military officers; they surrendered MacArthur, who was lodged in the gaol. The court broke up, and the officers then wrote to Bligh, accusing the Provost-Marshal of perjury in stating that they contemplated a rescue.

This business had lasted from the opening of the court in the morning until two o'clock in the afternoon.

Bligh, in accordance with his legal right, had all along refused to interfere with the constitution of the court. At the same time, there was no doubt that MacArthur could not have a fair trial if Judge-Advocate Atkins was to try him, for it was notorious that the two men had been at enmity for several years. Bligh demanded all the papers in the case from the officers, who, in his opinion, had illegally formed themselves into a court. They refused to give them up unless the governor appointed a new Judge-Advocate, and Bligh replied with a final demand that they should obey or refuse in writing. Then he wrote to Major Johnston, who commanded the regiment, and who lived some distance from Sydney, to come into town at once, as he wanted to see him over the "peculiar circumstances." Johnston sent a verbal message to the effect that he was too ill to come, or even to write. This was mere trickery.

1808

The next morning, January 26th (the anniversary of the founding of the colony), the officers assembled in the court-room, and as no prisoner was forthcoming for them to try, they wrote a protest to the governor, in which they set forth that, having been sworn in to try MacArthur, they conceived they could not break up the court until he was tried; that the accused had been arrested and removed from the court; and that, in effect, the sooner the governor appointed a new Judge-Advocate the better for all parties.

No notice was taken of this letter, but Bligh issued a summons to the officers to appear before him at Government House to answer for their conduct, and at the same time he wrote a second letter to Johnston, asking him to come to town, and got a second reply from that officer, to the effect that he was still too ill. But he was well enough to continue plotting against Bligh.

Soon after sending this second letter Johnston rode into town, arriving at the barracks at five o'clock in the evening. He held a consultation with his officers, and the upshot of this was that Johnston, as lieutenant-governor of the colony, demanded the instant release of MacArthur from gaol. The gaoler complied, and MacArthur went straight to the barracks, where a requisition to Johnston to place Bligh under arrest was arranged, at the suggestion of MacArthur, on the ground "that the present alarming state of the colony, in which every man's property, liberty, and life are endangered, induces us most earnestly to implore you instantly to assume the command of the colony. We pledge ourselves at a moment of less agitation to come forward to support the measure with our lives and fortunes." This was signed by several of the principal Sydney inhabitants, and then Johnston proceeded to carry out their and his own and the other rum-traffickers' designs.

The drums beat to arms; the New South Wales Corps—most of the men primed with the original cause of the trouble—formed in the barrack square, and with fixed bayonets, colours flying, and band playing, marched to Government House, led by Johnston.

It was about half-past six on an Australian summer evening, and broad daylight. The Government House guard waited to prime and load, then joined their drunken comrades, and the house was surrounded.

1808

Mrs. Putland, the governor's brave daughter (widow of a lieutenant in the navy, who had only been buried a week before), stood at the door, and endeavoured to prevent the soldiers from entering. She was pushed aside, and the house was soon full of soldiers, who, according to what some of them said, found Bligh hiding under his bed—a statement which, there is not the slightest doubt, was an infamous lie, suggested by the position in which the governor really was found, viz., standing behind a cot in a back room, where he was endeavouring to conceal some private papers.

Bligh surrendered to Johnston, who announced that he intended to assume the government "by the advice of all my officers and the most respectable of the inhabitants." Johnston caused Bligh's commission and all his papers to be sealed up, informed the governor that he would be kept a prisoner in his own house, and leaving a strong guard of soldiers, marched the rest of his inebriated command back to barracks, with the same parade of band-playing and pretence of dignity.

The colony was now practically under martial law, and Johnston appointed a new batch of civil officials, dismissing from office the others, including the Judge-Advocate, Atkins. MacArthur was then—humorously enough—tried by the court as newly constructed, and, of course, unanimously acquitted, Johnston then appointing him a magistrate and secretary of the colony. To complete the business, the court then took it upon themselves to try the Provost-Marshal, and gave him four months' gaol for having "falsely sworn that the officers of the New South Wales Corps intended to rescue his prisoner" (MacArthur), and at the same time the court sentenced the attorney who drew the indictment, and managed the legal business for Atkins, to a long term of imprisonment.

In July, Lieutenant-Colonel Foveaux arrived from England, and was surprised to find the existing state of affairs. By virtue of seniority, he succeeded Johnston as lieutenant-governor, and appointed another man in place of MacArthur, but did not interfere in any other way, contenting himself with sending to England a full report of the affair. Foveaux was in turn succeeded by Colonel Paterson, who arrived at the beginning of 1809, and who also declined to interfere in the business, but he granted Johnston leave of absence to proceed to England, MacArthur and two other officers accompanying him.

Meanwhile some of the free settlers had begun to show indications of a desire to help Bligh, who, to prevent accidents, was taken by the rebels from his house and lodged with his daughter a close prisoner in the barracks. Later on, he signed an agreement with Paterson to leave the colony for England in a sloop of war then bound home.

1809

Bligh and his daughter embarked on the vessel, but on the way she put into the Derwent river, in Van Diemen's Land, where the deposed governor landed, and at first thought he would be able to re-establish his authority, but the spirit of rebellion had taken hold; he was compelled to re-embark soon after, but he remained in Tasmanian waters on board ship until Governor Macquarie arrived from England.

For the English Government, in due course, had heard of the state of affairs, and woke up to the necessity for strong action. In December, 1809, there arrived in Sydney Harbour a 50-gun frigate and a transport, bringing Governor Macquarie, with his regiment of Highlanders, the 73rd. His orders were to restore Bligh for twenty-four hours and send home the New South Wales Corps, with every officer who had been concerned in the rebellion under arrest, and the regiment, as we said in a former chapter, was disbanded; Macquarie was himself then to take over the government.

The absence of Bligh from the colony prevented his restoration being literally carried out, but Macquarie issued proclamations which served the purpose, and restored all the officials who had been put out by the rebels. Macquarie soon made himself popular with the colonists, and the best proof of his success is the fact that he governed the colony for twelve years, and his administration, though an important epoch in its history, cannot be gone into here as he was not a naval man.

Bligh, the last of the naval governors, arrived in England in October, was made a rear-admiral, and died in 1817. Johnston was tried by court-martial and cashiered, and returned to the colony, becoming one of its best settlers and the founder of one of Sydney's most important suburbs. MacArthur was ordered not to return to the colony for eight years. He returned in 1817, bringing with him sons as vigorous as himself. Ultimately he became a member of the Legislative Council, and his services and those of his descendants will justly be remembered in Australia long after the petty annoyances to which he was subjected and the improper manner in which he resisted them have been totally and happily forgotten.

The history of Australia up to, and until the end of Bligh's appointment, can be summed up in half a dozen sentences. Phillip, during the term of his office, had repeatedly urged upon the home Government the necessity of sending out free men. Convicts without such a leaven could not, in his opinion, successfully lay the foundation of the "greatest acquisition England has ever made." Time proved the correctness of his judgment. The population of the colony, from something more than 1000 when he landed, had been increased at the close of King's administration to about 7000 persons. Half a dozen settlements had been formed at places within a few miles of Sydney; advantage had been taken of the discoveries of Bass and Flinders, and settlements made at Hobart and at Port Dalrymple; while an attempt (resulting in failure on this occasion and described later on) was made to colonize Port Phillip. A good deal of country was under cultivation, and stock had greatly increased, so that in the seventeen years that had elapsed some progress had been made, but the state of society at Botany Bay had grown worse rather than better. In the direction of reformation the experiment of turning felons into farmers was not a success. Few free emigrants had arrived in the colony, and those who came out were by no means the best class of people. Nobody worked more than they could help; drinking, gambling, and petty bickering occupied the leisure of most. This was the state of affairs which Captain Bligh was sent to reform, and we have seen how his mission succeeded.

In the case of the mutiny of the *Bounty*, it is reasonably believed that the mutineers were, at any rate, partially incited to their crime by the seductions of Tahiti; in the case of the revolt in New South Wales, it is known that allegiance to constituted authority had no part in the character of Bligh's subjects. Therefore, notwithstanding that Bligh was the victim of two outbreaks against his rule, posterity, without the most indisputable evidence to the contrary, would have held him acquitted of the least responsibility for his misfortunes. In the case of the *Bounty* mutiny the evidence of Bligh's opponents that the captain of the *Bounty* was a tyrannical officer remains uncontradicted by any authority but that of the *Bounty's* captain; in the case of the New South Wales revolt we can only judge of the probabilities, for the witnesses at the Johnston court-martial were of necessity upon one side. But the court-martial, a tribunal not at all likely to err upon the side of mutineers, came to the same conclusion as we have, and, so far as we are aware, most other writers acquainted with the subject have been driven to: that Bligh, to say the least of it, behaved with great indiscretion.

1829

Our references to this matter have been entirely to the minutes of the court-martial and to writers who wrote long enough ago to have had a personal knowledge of the subject or acquaintance with actors in the events. The lady whose letter we have quoted in the first pages of this chapter refers us to Lang's *History* for a justification of Bligh, and Dr. Lang, as is well known to students of Australian history, wrote more strongly in that governor's favour than did any other writer. Dr. Lang tells us that the behaviour of certain subordinates towards MacArthur was highly improper, and that MacArthur's speech in open court was "calculated to give great offence to a man of so exceedingly irritable disposition as Governor Bligh." Again, Dr. Lang says that Bligh by no means merited unqualified commendation for his government of New South Wales, and that the truth lies between the most unqualified praise and the most unqualified vituperation which the two sides of this quarrel have loaded upon his memory.

Judge Therry, who came to New South Wales in 1829, in a judicial summing up of the causes of this revolt, gives Bligh full credit for his attempt to govern well, and condemns in strong terms the outrageous conduct of the New South Wales Regiment; but he describes Bligh as a despotic man who "had proved his incapacity to govern a ship's crew whom he had driven to mutiny, yet had been made absolute ruler of a colony." Says Therry:—

"The extravagant and illegal proceedings to which these men" (the Judge-Advocate and his blackguard attorney) "had recourse contributed perhaps more than even the shortcomings of Bligh himself to the catastrophe that ensued. The governor's conflicts with many, but especially with MacArthur, were bitter and incessant through his career."

Says Dr. West, writing in 1852:—

1811

"The governor resolved to bring to trial the six officers, who had repelled the Judge-Advocate, for treasonable practices; and, as a preliminary step, ordered that they should appear before the bench of magistrates, of whom Colonel Johnston, their commander, was one. It was now supposed that Bligh intended to constitute a novel court of criminal jurisdiction, and that he had resolved to carry to the last extremes the hostility he had declared. Colonel Johnston, as a measure of self-defence, was induced to march his regiment to Government House, and place His Excellency under arrest, demanding his sword and his commission as governor. This transaction throughout caused a very strong sensation, both in the colony and at home. Opinions widely differ respecting its origin and its necessity. That it was illegal, it may be presumed, no one will deny; that it was wanton is not so indisputable. The unfortunate termination of Bligh's first expedition to Tahiti, the imputations of harshness and cruelty for ever fastened to his name, and the disreputable agents he sometimes employed in his service made the position of the officers extremely anxious, if not insecure. Bligh had become popular with the expired settlers, who reckoned a long arrear of vengeance to their military taskmasters, and who, with the law on their side or encouragement from the governor, might have been expected to show no mercy. Had Bligh escaped to the interior, the personal safety of the officers might have been imperilled. The settlers, led on by the undoubted representative of the Crown, would have been able to justify any step necessary for the recovery of his authority, and at whatever sacrifice of life."

The court-martial on Johnston was held at Chelsea Hospital, and lasted from May 11th till June 5th, 1811. Bligh complained that many of his papers had been stolen, and the want of these was detrimental to his case. Johnston, in the course of his defence, said:—

"My justification of my conduct depends upon my having proved to the satisfaction of this honourable court that such was the state of the public mind on the 26th of January, 1808, that no alternative was left for me but to pursue the measures I did or to have witnessed an insurrection and massacre in the colony, attended with the certain destruction of the governor himself. In doing this, I have endeavoured to show not only the fact of Captain Bligh's general unpopularity, and the readiness of the people to rise against him, and the probability that they would be joined by the soldiery, but also the causes of that unpopularity, founded on the general conduct of the governor."

The court came to the following decision:—

"The court having duly and maturely weighed and considered the whole of the evidence adduced on the prosecution, as well as what has been offered in defence, are of opinion that Lieutenant-Colonel Johnston is guilty of the act of mutiny as described in the charge, and do therefore sentence him to be cashiered";

and approval of the sentence is thus recorded:—

1811

"His Royal Highness the Prince Regent, in the name and on the behalf of His Majesty, was pleased, under all the circumstances of the case, to acquiesce in the sentence of the court. The court, in passing a sentence so inadequate to the enormity of the crime of which the prisoner has been found guilty, have apparently been actuated by a consideration of the novel and extraordinary circumstances which, by the evidence on the face of the proceedings, may have appeared to them to have existed during the administration of Governor Bligh, both as affecting the tranquillity of the colony and calling for some immediate decision. But although the Prince Regent admits the principle under which the court have allowed the consideration to act in mitigation of the punishment which the crime of mutiny would otherwise have suggested, yet no circumstances whatever can be received by His Royal Highness in full extenuation of an assumption of power so subversive of every principle of good order and discipline as that under which Lieutenant-Colonel Johnston has been convicted."

If Bligh had no part in bringing these disasters upon himself, he was a very unfortunate man (he was never given another command), and his enemies were extremely lucky in coming off so well. Mutineers whom he accused of taking active part against him, instead of getting hanged, rise to high rank in the service of the King; the military leader of an insurrection, in place of being shot on a parade-ground, is mildly dismissed the service, and becomes a prosperous settler upon the soil on which he raised the standard of revolution. But, whatever may have been his faults, arising from his ungovernable temper and arbitrary disposition, the statements of his military traducers reflecting on his personal courage may be dismissed with the contempt they deserve.

CHAPTER XII.

OTHER NAVAL PIONEERS, AND THE PRESENT MARITIME STATE OF AUSTRALIA—CONCLUSION.

1793

Long after Bligh, the last naval governor, was in his grave, the pioneer work of naval officers went on; and if not the chief aid to the settlement of Australia, it played an important part in its development. Begun at the foundation of the colony, when the marine explorer did his work in open boats; carried on, as the settlement grew, in locally built fore-and-aft vessels down to the present, when navigating officers are year in, year out, cruising "among the South Sea Islands," or on the less known parts of the northern and western Australian coast-line, surveying in up-to-date triple-expansion-engined steam cruisers or in steam surveying yachts, the work of chart-making has always been, and still is, done so thoroughly as to command the admiration of all who understand its its meaning, and withal so modestly that the shipmaster, whose Admiralty charts are perhaps little less or even more valuable to him than his Bible, scarcely ever thinks, if he knows, how they are made.

In the earliest days of the colony, Phillip and Hunter were land as well as sea explorers; Dawes and Tench, of the Marines, and Quartermaster Hacking, of the *Sirius*, in 1793 and 1794, made the first attempts to cross the Blue Mountains. Shortlands (father and son), Ball, of the *Supply*, and half a dozen other naval lieutenants, all made discoveries of importance; Vancouver, McClure, and Bligh (the latter twelve years before he was thought of as a governor) each did a share of early charting.

The list might be extended indefinitely. Let us take only one or two names and tell their stories; and these examples, with the narrative of Flinders and Bass, must stand as illustrative of the work of all.

In land exploring the military officers were not behindhand. Beside the work of the marines, a young Frenchman, Francis Louis Barrallier, an ensign of the New South Wales Corps, who came out with King, distinguished himself. King made him artillery and engineer officer, and he did much surveying with Grant in the *Lady Nelson*. Inland he went west until stopped by the Blue Mountains barrier; and King tells us an amusing story of this trip. Paterson, in command of the regiment, told King that he could not spare Barrallier for exploring purposes, so King, to get over the difficulty, appointed him his aide-de-camp, and then sent him on an "embassy to the King of the Mountains."

Barrallier went home in 1804, and saw a great deal of service in various regiments, distinguishing himself in military engineering, among his works being the erection of Nelson's column in Trafalgar Square. He died in London in 1853.

The *Lady Nelson* was a little brig of 60 tons burden, one of the first built with a centre-board, or sliding keels, as the idea was then termed. She was designed by Captain Schanck, one of the naval transport commissioners, and when she sailed from Portsmouth to begin her survey service in Australia, she was so deeply laden for her size that she had less than three feet of freeboard.

1800

Lieutenant James Grant was, through the influence of Banks, appointed to command this little vessel. He has much to say on the subject of sliding keels, for which see his *Narrative of a Voyage of Discovery*. The *Lady Nelson* was well built, and Grant showed his respect for her designer by his naming of Cape Schanck in Victoria and Mount Schanck in South Australia. In one of his letters to Banks, Grant says that, with all his stores of every description on board, he could take his vessel into seven feet of water, and could haul off a lee shore, by the use of sliding keels, "equal to any ship in the navy." On the night of January 23rd, 1800, it blew such a gale in the Channel that six vessels went on shore, and several others were reported missing. This gale lasted for nine days, and during that time the *Lady Nelson* rode comfortably at her anchor in the Downs.

Grant's instructions when he left England were to proceed through the newly discovered Bass' Straits on his way, report himself at Sydney, and then set to work and survey the coast, beginning with the southern and south-western parts of it. The brig sailed, with a crew of seventeen all told, in February, 1800, and arrived on December 16th of the same year, being the first vessel to pass through Bass' Straits on the way from England to Australia. On the voyage Grant discovered and named many points on the Victorian coast-line; then, as soon as the vessel arrived and received a thorough overhaul, she was sent to sea again to continue the work in company with a small intercolonial vessel, the *Bee*.

They sailed on March 8th, 1801, and were surveying until May 2nd, when Grant sums up the work done in these words:—

> "We have now gained a complete survey of the coast from Western Point to Wilson's Promontory, with the situation of the different islands of the same, and ascertained the latitudes of the same, which from our different observations we have been able to do sufficiently correct . . . These points being ascertained so far as lays in our power, I judge it most prudent to make the best of our way to port, keeping the shore well in sight to observe every particular hitherto unknown."

1801

The portions left out in this extract refer to the latitudes and longitudes, which are so correctly given that the only ascertainable difference between them and the figures in a recent addition of Norrie is in the case of Wilson's Promontory, which Grant says is in longitude between 146° 25' and 146° 14', and Norrie's table gives us 146° 25' 37".

On the return of the little vessel, she took part in an interesting ceremony, which the following proclamation by Governor King, dated May 29th, best describes:—

"Thursday next being the anniversary of His Majesty's birth, will be observed as a holyday. The present Union will be hoisted at sunrise. At a quarter before nine the New South Wales Corps and Association to be under arms, when the Royal Proclamation for the Union between Great Britain and Ireland will be publicly read by the Provost-Marshall, and on the New Union flag being displayed at Dawes Point and on board His Majesty's armed vessel *Lady Nelson* the military will fire three rounds, which the batteries will take up, beginning at the main guard, Bennilong and Dawes Points, at the Windmill Hills, and at the barracks. When finished, His Majesty's armed vessel the *Lady Nelson* will fire 21 guns, man ship, and cheer. At noon the salute will be repeated from the batteries, New South Wales Corps and Association will fire three rounds, and at one o'clock the *Lady Nelson* will fire 21 guns in honour of His Majesty's birthday. The Governor will be ready to receive the compliments of the officers, civil and military, on those happy occasions, at half-past one o'clock."

King had a high opinion of Grant as a seaman, but he considered him an unscientific man, not suitable for surveying, and wrote to England to that effect. Grant himself confirms this in a letter asking to go home, as from the "little knowledge I have of surveying, . . . where I may be enabled to be more serviceable to my country." His faith in sliding keels had been somewhat shaken by this time, and he complained that he could not claw his vessel off a lee shore, and so Flinders found, when Grant with the *Lady Nelson* kept him company along the Barrier Reef when the *Investigator* was surveying that part of the coast. The *Nelson* had been ordered to act as tender to the *Investigator*, but she was so unsuited to the work that Flinders lost patience and sent her back to Sydney, where she did a great deal of surveying in the exploration of the Hunter River and its vicinity. Grant went home, and cut a much better figure as a fighting officer, was promoted commander, and died in 1838. On his way home he took a box of King's despatches to convey to England, and when the despatch-box was opened it was found to be empty. King, writing of this matter, said:—

1802

"I do not blame Lieutenant Grant so much for the villainous transaction respecting the loss of my despatches as I deprecate the infamy of those who had preconcerted the plan. Before the vessel he went in left the colony, it was told me that such an event would happen, and the master's conduct prior to his leaving this fully justified the report. I would not suffer the vessel to leave the port before a bond of £500 was given that neither Lieutenant Grant or the despatches should be molested. Under these circumstances and Lieutenant Grant's knowledge of the master, he ought to have been more guarded, as I gave my positive directions that the vessel should be seen a certain way to sea, and the box was not given from my possession before the vessel was under way. However, the plan was too well laid and bound with ill-got gold to fail. Let the villain enjoy the success of his infamy. As to any publication of Mr. Grant's, I believe nothing new or original can arise from his pen without the aid of auxiliary fiction."

Lieutenant Murray, of the *Porpoise*, relieved Grant in the *Lady Nelson*, and Murray and his mate. Lieutenant Bowen, further explored Bass' Straits and the Victorian coast, their chief achievement being the discovery of Port Phillip.

The *Lady Nelson* was off the heads of Port Phillip on January 5th, 1802, but the weather was too bad to enter, and Bowen was sent to examine the bay in one of the brig's boats. This he did, and the *Lady Nelson* entered, and anchored off what is now the quarantine station on February 15th. Murray took possession of the place on March 9th, naming it Port King, and Surveyor Grimes made a survey of it. They left on March 12th. The Frenchman Baudin, with the *Geographe* and *Naturaliste*, eighteen days later ran along this coast and claimed its discovery, although the Englishmen, Flinders in particular, had already surveyed and named nearly all his discoveries; but Baudin was gracious enough to admit that Port Phillip, which he had only sighted, had been first entered by the *Lady Nelson*. Flinders sailed into the bay on April 26th, thinking that he had made a new discovery, until, on his arrival at Port Jackson, he heard of the *Lady Nelson's* prior visit, and that Governor King, with modesty and regard for his old chief, had altered Murray's name of Port King to Port Phillip.

In consequence of Murray's services in the *Lady Nelson*, King appointed him acting lieutenant, and strongly recommended the Admiralty should confirm the appointment.

With the recommendation, Murray sent home, through the governor, the following certificate of his services, which is interesting as showing how such certificates were then written, and because of what came of this particular recommendation:—

"In pursuance of the directions of Sir Roger Curtis, Bart., Vice-Admiral of the White and Commander-in-chief of His Majesty's ships and vessels employed and to be employed at the Cape of Good Hope and the seas adjacent, dated the 8th July, 1800. "We have examined Mr. John Murray, who appears to be more than 21 years of age, and has been at sea more than six years in the ships and qualities undermentioned, viz.:—

Ships.	Entry.	Quality.	Discharge.	Y.	M.	W.	D.
Duke	9 June, 1789	Able Seaman	2 Dec., 1789	...	5	2	2
Polyphemus	10 Oct., 1794	Midshipman	7 May, 1797	2	7	2	...
Apollo	8 May, 1797	Mate	27 Dec., 1797	...	8	1	3
Blazer	2 Jan., 1798	2nd Master and Pilot	26 July, 1798	...	7	1	3
Porpoise	7 Oct.,1798	Mate	9 July, 1800	1	9	...	...
				6	1	3	1

"He produceth journals kept by himself in the *Polyphemus, Apollo*, and *Porpoise*, and certificates from Captains Lumsdine, Manly, and Scott, of his diligence and sobriety. He can splice knots, reef and sail, work a ship in sailing, and shift his tides, keep a reckoning of the ship's way by plain sailing and Mercator, observe the sun and stars, and find the variation of the compass, and is qualified to do the duty of an able seaman and midshipman.

"Given under our hands on His Majesty's ship *Adamant*, in Simon's Bay, Cape of Good Hope, this 9th day of July, 1800.

J. Motham,	Captains of	*Adamant,*
Thomas Larcom, }	His Majesty's {	*Lancaster,*
Roger Curtis,	ships	*Rattlesnake.*

The Secretary to the Admiralty wrote to Governor King on May 5th, 1802, stating that this passing certificate of Mr. Murray's was "an imposition attempted to be practised in his report of services, and to acquaint you that they will not, in consequence, give him a commission, nor will they allow him to pass for an officer at any future period." With this letter came an enclosure showing that by Mr. Murray's passing certificate "it is set forth that he served in the *Duke* from the 9th June, 1789, to the 2nd December, 1789, but we must observe that the *Duke* was not in commission in 1789, neither is he found on her books from the 10th of August, 1790, to 2nd August, 1791, when she was in commission, nor is he born on the *Duke* while she was in ordinary, which time, even admitting he did belong to her, would not have been allowed towards the regular servitude of six years."

1803

In reply to this charge, Murray told King that he could "explain" the circumstance; but he soon after returned to England, and these deponents can find no further trace of him.

Soon after it was decided to colonize the new discovery, and the *Calcutta*, man-of-war, and *Ocean*, transport, sailed from Portsmouth with prisoners and stores on April 26th, 1803, arriving at Port Phillip on October 10th. Collins, now a brevet-lieutenant-colonel, who was Judge-Advocate under Phillip, was in command of the expedition, and was to be the first governor of the settlement.

King, at Port Jackson, had meanwhile sent—in May, 1803—Lieutenant Bowen in the *Lady Nelson,* with a transport and a party of settlers, to form a settlement at the head of the Derwent in Van Diemen's Land.

The expedition was made up of 307 male convicts, 17 of their wives, and 7 children; 4 officers and 47 non-commissioned officers and men of the Marines, with 5 women and 1 child; and a party of 11 men and 1 woman, free settlers. Besides these were about 12 civilian officials. By the close of 1803, Collins, with the concurrence of most, if not all, of his officers, decided to abandon Port Phillip, and convey his colonists to the Derwent settlement. His justification for taking this step was the unsuitableness of the land and the difficulty of procuring fresh water near the heads of Port Phillip. This shows that he was not of the same spirit as Governor Phillip, and that he wrote history far better than he made it.

Bowen had already begun the settlement near what was named Hobart Town by him in honour of the Secretary of State, Lord Hobart. In 1881 the "Town" was dropped, and "Hobart" became the official name of the capital of Tasmania. The man acting as mate of the *Lady Nelson* was one Jorgenson, the "King of Iceland," whose remarkable story was written by Mr. Hogan, and published by Ward and Downey in 1891, and whose career was a most extraordinary series of adventures. The *Lady Nelson* pursued her careful and useful voyages until 1827, when she was seized by Maoris on the coast of New Zealand and destroyed.

1822

In 1817 there came out young Phillip Parker King, son of Governor King, who made four voyages round the Australian coast, completing a minute survey in 1822, when he returned to England and published an interesting account of his work. Sir Gordon Bremer in the *Tamar*, Sterling in the *Success*, Fitzroy in the *Beagle*, Hodson in the *Rattlesnake*, Captain (afterwards Sir George) Grey on the West Australian coast, Blackwood in the *Fly*, Stokes and Wickham, and scores of other naval officers ought to be mentioned, and no attempt can be made in a work like this to do justice to the merchantmen who, in whalers and sealers or East Indiamen, in a quiet, modest, business-like way of doing the thing, sailed about the coast making discoveries, and often, through the desertion of their seamen, leading to the foundation of settlements.

Gregory Blaxland, William Lawson, and William Charles Wentworth, in Governor Macquarie's time, were the first men to make an appreciable advance to the west, inland from the sea. Lawson was a lieutenant in the New South Wales Corps, in the Veteran Company of which notorious regiment he remained attached to the 73rd when the "Botany Bay Rangers" went home. Blaxland was an early settler in the colony, and Wentworth was the son of a wealthy Norfolk Island official, who had sent his boy home to be educated, and when these three men went exploring, young Wentworth had just returned to Australia. In 1813, after many hard trials, by keeping to the crown of the range and avoiding the impenetrable gorges which their predecessors had thought would lead to a pass through the barrier, they managed to gain the summit of the main range, and then returned to Sydney. The work had taken a month to perform, and Macquarie promptly sent out a fully equipped party to follow up the discovery. So thoroughly did the governor back up the work of the explorers that by January, 1815, the convict-made road had been completed to Bathurst, and the Blue Mountain ranges were no longer a barrier to the good country of the west.

The Humes, Evans, Oxley, and the rest of the land explorers followed as the years went on, and very soon there was not a mile of undiscovered land in the mother-colony. Attempts to penetrate the interior of the great continent followed, and that work and the opening of the far north, with its too often accompaniments of disaster and death, went on until quite recent times. Occasionally even now we hear much talk of expeditions into the interior, but newspaper-readers who read of such exploring parties can generally take it for granted that stories of hazard and hardship nowadays lose nothing in the telling, especially where mining interests and financial speculation are concerned.

By way of ending to this story of the naval pioneers of Australia, it will perhaps be not amiss to show what the navy was in Australia at the beginning of the century and what it is now at its close. A return issued by Governor King on the 4th of August, 1804, showed that the *Buffalo*, ship of war, with a crew of 84 men, the *Lady Nelson*, a 60-ton brig, with 15 men, were the only men-of-war that could be so described on the station. The *Investigator*, Flinders' ship, was then being patched up to go home, and she is stated to have 26 men rated on her books. Belonging to the Colonial Government were the *Francis*, a 40-ton schooner, the *Cumberland*, 20-ton schooner, the *Integrity*, a cutter of 59 tons, the *Resource*, a schooner of 26 tons, built from the wrecks of the *Porpoise* and *Cato*, and some punts and open boats. The crews of all these vessels amounted to 145 men.

A return dated six months later shows that there were 23 merchant vessels owned, or constantly employed, in the colony, of a total tonnage of 660 tons, carrying crews numbering altogether 117. The vessels varied in size from the *King George*, of 185 tons and 25 men, to the *Margaret*, of 7 tons and 2 men.

In the year 1898 the royal naval forces in Australian waters make a squadron, under the command of a rear-admiral, consisting of 17 ships. Of these 15 (including 3 surveying vessels at present attached to the Australian station) are in commission, and 2 in reserve. The total tonnage of the vessels in commission and in reserve amounts to 31,795 tons, armed with the most modern weapons, and carrying crews numbering in the aggregate about 3000, while the naval establishment at Garden Island (so called because about a hundred and twenty years ago it was used as a vegetable garden for the crew of the *Sirius*) is now one of the most important British naval stations.

Seven of these war vessels belong to a special squadron, the maintenance of which is partially paid for by the colonial governments; and, by agreement with the Imperial Government, the ships are to be employed in Australasian waters solely for the defence of Australia and New Zealand. Besides this force, most of the colonial governments maintain a naval reserve of their own, highly efficient, perhaps, as a land force, but, owing to the lack of vessels and of money, scarcely to be considered seriously of value as a naval defence force.

The merchant shipping trade of Australia, measured by the entering and clearing returns from all Australian ports, now reaches about 18,000,000 tons annually, of which about one-third is entered or cleared from the ports of the mother-colony. The returns do not separate purely local tonnage from the other shipping of the British empire, but out of the above 18,000,000 tons some 16,000,000 tons are classed as British, and Australia as a whole contributes no mean proportion of that amount.

Here ends this account of the naval pioneers of Australia. We have already said that this work is biographical rather than historical. All that we have attempted is not to sketch the progress of the colony—as a colony, for the first twenty years of its existence, no element of progress was in it—but to show how certain naval officers, in spite of the difficulties of the penal settlement days, in spite very often of their own unfitness for this to them strange service, did their work well, not perhaps always governing wisely, but holding to ground won in such circumstances and by such poor means as men with more brains and less "grit" would have abandoned as untenable.

Arthur Phillip landed in a desert, obtained a footing on the land, and when he left it, left behind him a habitable country; Hunter and King followed him and held the country, though nearly every man's hand was against them, and the industrious and the virtuous among their people could be numbered by the fingers of the hand. Yet these men and their officers dotted the coast-line with their discoveries, and by what they wrought in the direction of sea exploration more than made up for what they lacked in the art of civil governing. Bligh honestly endeavoured in a blundering way to accomplish that which only the sharp lesson of his mistake made possible; Macquarie, backed by a regiment, began his administration with concessions, and continued for many years to govern the colony, chiefly for the benefit of the emancipists instead of for its officials. Whatever evils may have come of his methods, it has been said of him that "he found a garrison and a gaol, and left the broad and deep foundations of an empire." Such foundation was really laid by his successors, who encouraged the emigration of free men who presently demanded that Australia should no longer be used as a place of punishment, and its lands as a reward for felons; that it must be a British colony in the fullest and freest sense. It is to these men, marching forward upon ways cut for them by the naval pioneers, we owe the fulfilment of Phillip's prediction that "this would be the most valuable acquisition England ever made."

BIBLIOBAZAAR

The essential book market!

Did you know that you can get any of our titles in large print?

Did you know that we have an ever-growing collection of books in many languages?

Order online:
www.bibliobazaar.com

Find all of your favorite classic books!

Stay up to date with the latest government reports!

At BiblioBazaar, we aim to make knowledge more accessible by making thousands of titles available to you- *quickly and affordably*.

Contact us:
BiblioBazaar
PO Box 21206
Charleston, SC 29413